Also available from
Natalie Charles

Archer Cove Series
The Coffee Girl
A Sweet Possibility

Harlequin Romantic Suspense
The Seven-Day Target
The Burden of Desire
When No One Is Watching

Natalie Charles

A Winter Promise

◆Cranberry Press◆

ISBN-13: 978-0-9862805-4-2

A WINTER PROMISE

Cover design: Ebooklaunch.com
Copy Editor: Amanda Sumner
Proofreader: Carol Carlisle Agnew

For Ryan

"I knew when I met you an adventure was going to happen." — A. A. Milne

A WINTER PROMISE

CHAPTER ONE

ANNA TUMBLESBY INHALED deeply and tugged at the furry white hem of her dress. Downstairs in the lobby of the Archer Cove Inn, a camera crew was setting up in front of the roaring fire. Fair Isle stockings were hung across the stone fireplace with care, and fresh garland was strung through the banister leading to the second floor, held in place by red velvet bows. Downstairs, her sister Charis was probably enjoying a cup of peppermint tea. But upstairs in room 202, Anna was freaking the heck out.

In her thirty-six years on the planet — not including any past lives — Anna had come to recognize two truths. The first: natural toothpaste made with baking soda and essential oils did not clean her teeth. The second: the holidays? Not her thing.

She couldn't quite put her finger on why. It was all nice enough, what with the lights and the brightly colored gifts. The food was great, certainly. Anna could get behind a plate of Christmas cookies and a tumbler of eggnog, and that's where she found herself at most festive events. But she'd never managed to feel the outpouring of excitement that she was expected to feel at that time of year. To her, the holidays were just another list of social events and obligations. Fortunately, she was pretty good at faking it.

"Hello, I'm Anna Tumblesby, and I think the holidays are magical." Anna smiled brightly at her reflection, paused, and then glanced over her shoulder. "Too cheesy?"

"Uh, a bit." Anna's youngest sister, Flossie, was lying flat on her back on the four-poster bed, her gray-stockinged feet resting on the top of the headboard. "You sound like you're hosting a Christmas spectacular or something. You know, with tap-dancing elves and candy canes with jazz hands." She was staring straight at the ceiling, but she fluttered her hands to demonstrate. "Don't tell Charis I said that. She'll get ideas."

Their sister Charis was the one who love love *loved* the holidays. Always had. As a child, she was cast in the Archer Cove Thanksgiving Parade as Little Miss Christmas for four years straight, where she got to sit in Santa's sleigh and throw candy to onlookers. These days she was onto bigger and better things, like planning the Archer Cove Holiday Festival. After years of nagging, she'd finally managed to rope Anna in as her festival co-chair, a role Anna had regretted accepting every day since.

"In fairness to me," Anna said, "I *am* hosting a Christmas spectacular. Sort of. An interfaith Christmas spectacular." She tugged her silver hoop earring free of her hair and made a mental note not to repeat the words "interfaith Christmas" for the cameras. It was the kind of statement that would make her look foolish and win a long sigh from Sandy Thane, the prune-mouthed chair of the Chamber of Commerce.

Blame it on the winter doldrums, or the anxiety of facing another holiday season alone in the large, old inn. Anna needed to be busy — always had. In the three years since she'd first come to own the inn, Anna had become accustomed to its rhythms. She was busiest beginning in the late spring and continuing through early fall. There was a slowdown until the leaves changed and business burst again, and then an interminable stretch of quiet. She barely knew what to do with herself when only a few rooms were filled.

That year, Anna had finally decided that instead of sitting around the inn gathering cobwebs, she would assist Charis with planning the holiday festivities. A town-wide cookie swap. Caroling down Main Street. A Jingle Bell Dance at the community center. Basically, the same old festivities that had been planned for as long as Anna could remember. Sandy had appointed Anna co-chair of the Festival Planning Committee, but had promptly vetoed all of her new ideas. "Ice skating? What if it's too warm? And the sheer *liability*." She shook her head disapprovingly. "I'm afraid we can't risk it."

In the midst of planning, Charis had secured a local news segment and appointed Anna the official spokesperson for the event. "You're so much better at these things than I am, Anna," she'd said, tilting her head slightly to deliver the compliment. "The cameras love you, and who knows? Maybe you'll drum up some business for the inn."

The only problem was...*her*. Anna was a behind-the-scenes kind of gal. When she got nervous, she jumbled her words and everything came out all wrong. It all went back to her first stage appearance in the second grade Thanksgiving play. For some reason, blonde, blue-eyed Anna had been cast as a Native American, and she had one line: "I brought the maize." When the time came for her to walk onstage, Anna promptly peed her pants and ran in the other direction.

She watched Flossie in the mirror. "We're being profiled on *Connecticut Sunrise*. I have to come up with something to say." Preferably something brilliant and memorable.

"Have fun with it." Flossie reached up to grab her toes. "Why don't you keep it simple and just say, 'Hi, I'm Anna. Welcome to the Holly Jolly Bullpen.'"

Yes, that was how they had been secretly referring to the inn. It was holly jolly headquarters for the officially named "Festival in the Cove." But "Holly Jolly Bullpen" was used as a joke between her and Flossie. No one else would understand. "I can't say that," Anna replied. "It would undermine the dignity of the piece."

That got her little sister's attention. Flossie rolled to one side without bothering to lift her head. "Did you say 'dignity'? You're wearing an elf suit."

Anna's hands flew to the green crushed velvet of her dress. The hem fell halfway down her thighs and was tinged with white faux fur. Her waist was cinched with a wide black leather belt with an enormous gold buckle. Charis had selected it and assured her that it was perfect for the news segment. "It's not an elf suit," Anna replied. "Just because it's festive..."

Plus, would an elf suit reveal her cleavage so flatteringly? No, it would not. Would an elf suit make her legs look so good when paired with black ankle boots? Case closed. This was a fun, holiday-themed dress. She could easily wear it to any cocktail party. "Maybe it's a little ironic," Anna ventured.

"Yeah, it's an elf suit. Ironically, you're wearing it as a dress." Flossie sat up on the bed, tousled her long, strawberry-blonde hair, and yawned. "How long is this going to take, anyway? I want to take a nap." It was eight o'clock in the morning.

There was a knock at the door. "Yes?" Anna called.

"Miss Tumblesby? We have your mic."

"Come in."

The door opened and a small, wiry woman with close-cropped brown hair rushed in. "This will just take a minute," she said, and paused. "Do you mind if I unzip your dress a little?"

"No, go ahead." Anna pulled her long blonde curls to one shoulder and glanced at Flossie in the mirror. "You don't have to be here. If you're tired."

Flossie raised her shoulders halfheartedly. "It's fun. I'll be morally supportive. And there's nowhere I'd rather be today than in the Holly Jolly Bullpen." The sisters exchanged a smile in the mirror.

Once the microphone was fitted, they were ready. Show's about to begin, Anna thought. There was no turning back. No peeing herself. It was time to bring the maize.

Anna's limbs trembled as she walked down the stairs. Members of the town had come out to view the taping, and a few clapped when they saw her. Flossie giggled beside her. "Oooh, you're going to be famous."

"Anna! Oh my. You look *amazing*!"

Anna turned to see Charis's little sparrow-like figure bobbing excitedly. She may have been in her thirties, but Charis was still Little Miss Christmas. Exhibit one: her candy cane earrings. Anna forced a broad but shaky smile. "Hey. Thanks. You don't think I look like an elf?"

"Oh my goodness, no! You look adorable, and your aura is brilliant blue! Oh, and I brought some children with me," Charis said, gripping Anna's wrist between her warm fingers. "I hope you don't mind."

She'd brought...children? Oddly, it didn't surprise Anna. "No, of course not. The more the merrier."

"They're orphans," Charis whispered. (Of course they were.) "Children from the state-run home, poor darlings. The foster care system... I can't even talk about it. They could use a little Christmas cheer. We all could." She tilted her head and nodded solemnly. "I rented a bus. They're all so excited. There are a few counselors, too. To keep them away from sharp objects. And also because one of the little girls starts fires, bless her heart."

Anna sucked a breath as Charis's voice finally came to a halt. "Great," she exhaled. "Well, keep them away from the fireplace, I guess. And the kitchen."

"Oh, don't you worry." She leaned in closer, and Anna smelled cinnamon on her breath. "You just go on up there and make us proud! We'll all be watching."

No pressure there.

Anna's attention turned to Devon Gail, the journalist who would be interviewing her. Devon had her arms outstretched and was waiting while someone from wardrobe pinned her gray jacket in place for a more tailored look. Anna admired her dark skin and bright smile with a pang. Devon was gorgeous. Beside her, she was going to look about as attractive as forgotten leftovers.

"Anna." Devon beamed warmly, lowering her arms to clasp Anna's hands. "What a beautiful inn. So pretty and quaint. I'm really looking forward to our chat."

"Me too," Anna said, lying just a little bit.

Devon touched a finger lightly to her short, chic curls and ran a gaze down Anna's figure. "I love that dress. It's precious."

But something in her tone made Anna feel self-conscious. She'd opted for holiday festive. Devon had not. Anna adjusted the fabric around the belt. "Thank you."

A man approached them and explained what was going to happen. They had already taken a number of shots of the property and the town, and they'd done preliminary interviews to get the background. "Anna, Devon's going to ask you some questions about the festival," he explained. "It's going to be real low-key."

"We'll keep it conversational," Devon added. "Nothing to be nervous about. This is a feel-good piece."

Anna's mouth had gone dry, so she nodded and said, "Uh huh."

The crew had set two director chairs in front of the fireplace. Anna waited for Devon to take her seat before climbing into her chair. As she waited for the cue to begin, Anna took a deep breath and tried to relax. This was going to be fantastic publicity for the inn. A local television segment! She could be fully booked before the day was up. As someone adjusted the lights, she reminded herself to smile and enjoy. But then she felt the weight of everything that was resting on the interview: an inn filled with guests at the holidays. Could she be so lucky?

And suddenly, Devon had started. She smiled easily at the camera and leaned forward engagingly. "What do you think of when you think of the perfect holiday season? Ice skating and marshmallows? Sleigh bells in the snow? We're here in the idyllic town of Archer Cove, Connecticut, where one innkeeper is on a mission to create warm winter memories for the townspeople."

Anna's spine went rigid as Devon spun toward her. Relax, she told herself. Remember to breathe. Devon's smile was warm as sunshine as she said, "Anna, you've created the loveliest winter festival. Can you tell us a little bit about it?"

Shoot, her mouth was bone dry, and she could hear her own tongue unsticking itself as she attempted to answer. "The holidays...are a magical time," she began, a little breathlessly. "I've always loved the idea of families gathering together, and the contrast of snow and warmth. I wanted to create a winter like you'd see in a painting — er, a postcard."

"And of course this brings in visitors, too," Devon added. "That must be good for business."

Anna started at the implication. "Y-yes, but it's not just about that. If people from out of town come to the inn to enjoy the festivities, that's a bonus."

She licked her lips with a dry tongue, desperate to explain herself. This wasn't about money, she was sure of it. This was about staying busy, being active. Being surrounded by people and not left with her own thoughts. But that wasn't the kind of thing one confessed to a journalist in front of television cameras. *Hello, I'm Anna Tumblesby, and I'm desperately lonely.*

She opted for a change of subject. "We have a whole schedule of activities lined up. I'm terribly excited about the cookie swap. There will be an award for the best cookie, of course —"

Anna's words trailed as the corner of her eye caught a flash of movement. A man had just entered the inn and was walking down the makeshift side aisle of the viewing audience. He paused just on the edge of the shadows, but Anna saw him clearly enough, and froze.

She was barely aware of a stretch of silence, and then Devon cleared her throat. "So there will be a cookie contest, then?" she prompted. "That sounds like a lot of fun! How does that work, exactly?"

But Anna's attention was still on the man who'd just entered. "Yes," she began slowly, allowing her eyes to move from Devon to the visitor. "There will be marshmallows."

Shoot. Was that really him? Did he actually have the unmitigated gall? Anna's mind unraveled as Devon shuffled some papers in her lap and gave a dry laugh. "I understand you and your sister have a special term for the inn during this festive time. Do you want to share what that is?"

They'd done a pre-interview with Flossie? She'd never mentioned that. "Oh." Anna forced a burst of laughter. "We call it the Holly Jolly Bull Penis. It's just a private joke."

With a swift whoosh, the air left the room. Devon's eyes widened, and she looked back down at her lap. Anna glanced out over the faces in the audience and the realization slowly hit. "Sorry," she murmured, teasing the fur trim on her dress again. "Did I say — ? Bullpen. Holly Jolly Bullpen. Because, um, it's about a baseball reference? And just, you know, warm up. Warming up. There's the fireplace."

Well, there she went, headfirst off the cliff. It was a long, slow fall from here. Anna clenched her eyes shut and gripped her dress. "Um, would you mind if I...could I get a glass of drink? Not a drink. Alcohol, I mean." She exhaled. "Just water. My mouth is dry."

Devon blinked and her smile tightened. "We're live."

"Oh." Anna's cheeks burned. "Right. I forgot about that."

"It happens to the best of us." The reporter crossed one slender leg over the other and leaned closer to Anna. "You know, you must love the holidays to invest so much of yourself in this festival. Can you tell me about your favorite holiday tradition?"

"I don't...know."

Anna stared at the camera lens. Wires were coiled like snakes around the floor — what if someone tripped? Would she be sued for that? And Devon wanted to know what she loved so much about the holidays, and why wouldn't Anna's mouth work? Blast.

Beside her, Devon laughed good-naturedly and shuffled her papers again. "So, it could be anything. Like a favorite food, or a toy you received —"

"The holidays are kind of a hard time for me," Anna said quietly. Her voice sounded strained and thin to her ears. "I didn't plan this festival because I wanted money. I planned it because I don't want to be alone. Because if I'm busy, then I can forget."

She was staring at her fists as she spoke, clenching and unclenching them on her lap. As she finished speaking, she brought her gaze up to meet Devon's, and she saw that she'd said the wrong thing. Again. "I'm sorry, Devon," Anna muttered. "I don't do well with perky small talk. I just said 'bull penis' in front of the orphans. And on live television." There was a burst of giggles in the audience, but Anna continued. "Look, it's going to be a nice festival. We kick off in two weeks with hot chocolate and cookies at the inn. Everyone's welcome. Maybe you love the holidays, or maybe you find them sad and stressful and they remind you of the passage of time and make you want to lose your feelings in a container of that orange popcorn that people like to send around this time of year. You know what I mean? That cheese popcorn that's covered with orange dust. It comes in the tin. Either way, you're welcome to attend the festival. We'd love to have you."

She paused, and her ears were filled with only the sound of her own thundering heart and a crackle as a log slipped in the fireplace. That camera was still pointed at her. Anna pressed her lips together and turned to Devon. "Anyway, the cookie making competition isn't limited to cookies. I hope participants will feel free to make brownies and other things, too. Oh, and the Jingle Bell Dance requires a sign-up! But it's posted on our website." She smiled. "If you're coming from out of town, there's plenty of time."

She folded her hands in her lap to signal that the interview had ended — and on a decent note, all things considered. Devon's lovely face had gone blank and her jaw slack, but she recovered after a beat and glanced at the producer. "Well, a few minutes early. But we're okay, right, Tom?"

Anna didn't wait for the answer before rising and shuffling off the set toward the man who had entered. Behind her she heard Devon say, "I guess we'll all just take a break?"

Let them all scramble. Anna didn't care. The segment was mostly ruined, though maybe they'd give her a chance to do a quick follow-up, assuming she could manage to pull herself together in the next few minutes. But composure seemed less and less likely as she approached the man at the side of the room and his features came into focus. That thick, dark-blond hair. Those sharply blue eyes, intense and gentle at the same time. He had a beard, but she'd still recognize him anywhere. Her heart arrested. "Ben."

He was clearly waiting for her, but he hadn't yet made himself comfortable. He was still wearing a black winter jacket zipped all the way up to meet a black scarf. As if just realizing he was indoors beside a fire, Ben tugged at the zipper of his coat. "Hey, Anna." Casual, as if she should have been expecting him. "How's it going?"

She swallowed and took him in, still in disbelief. Finally she managed to say, "What are you doing here?"

"You're joking, right?" He smiled and his gaze softened. "I heard about the festival. It's been a long time." He looked behind her. "I hope I didn't interrupt."

Too late for all of that, Anna thought. She reached out and grasped his sleeve. "Come with me."

21

He obliged, stumbling after her as she wound them around the lengths of cords and random people, through the lobby and down the hall, back into the kitchen. Goodness, the kitchen was a mess! There were eggshells left on the white-and-gray granite island, and the stainless-steel appliances were covered in gummy fingerprints. Anna's thoughts immediately flew to Marian, the assistant she'd hired just three weeks ago. Big mistake, but she'd deal with that later. Right now, there were larger quiche to bake. Even so, as she released her grip on Ben's sleeve and spun on her heel to face him, the first words out of her mouth were, "I'm sorry for the mess."

It made him laugh quietly without dispelling any of the awkwardness between them. "I don't care about that."

She inhaled and then headed to the cabinet beside the sink to retrieve a glass. "You shouldn't be here. You...how long has it been? Six months? Longer? You need to leave. Please." She turned on the sink and filled the glass with water. "Whatever you want, we can talk about it later. On the phone." *Through our lawyers.*

His coat was fully unzipped, but his scarf was still wound around his neck. He stuffed his hands into the pockets of his jeans. "I'm staying here. I drove all the way from the city."

What the...what now? A trickle of water dribbled down Anna's chin. She reached for the red gingham towel balled beside the sink and wiped her face. Gah! She pulled it back. There were raw eggs on it. *Damn it.*

She flung the towel to the side. "I'm afraid we're all booked up. No room at the inn this Christmas." She smiled weakly at her own joke. "Too bad. There's a nice place over in Spencer —"

"I have a reservation," Ben said as he gathered the broken eggshells on the counter and dropped them into the trashcan.

"Oh, that's probably a mistake," she said quickly. "I have a new assistant, and she's not familiar with...computers. Or cleaning." *Or the unwritten "Do-Not-Book" list.* "This is sort of embarrassing for me, really. You're welcome to stay for brunch. On the house, of course. Because of the inconvenience."

But Ben wasn't buying it. "I have a reservation, Anna. A real one. I'm staying at the Holly Jolly Bullpen." He grinned. "That's a cute name, by the way. And I'm fixing the roof on one of the guest houses — didn't you know that? You hired me."

She most certainly had *not* hired Ben to fix the roof on the guest house. She hadn't hired anyone. In fact, she'd delegated that task to Flossie... Anna's blood pooled. *That sneak!*

Her hands flew to her hips and found the thick leather belt. "This is holly jolly bullshit, is what it is!"

She was in no way equipped to deal with this. Not standing in a messy kitchen, wearing...yes. An elf suit. She was dressed in an elf suit and she might as well just admit it. Though the neckline made her breasts look great. Still, Anna was not about to hash it out with Ben right then. "Tell me the truth: why are you here?"

"I told you the truth." He paused to face her, his broad shoulders slumping just slightly under her withering glare. "You're my wife. Why shouldn't I be here with you? It's the holidays."

So he still remembered they were married? Funny how memory could slip in and out so conveniently. "Mail that to months ago, Ben. I'm dressed like one of Santa's helpers, and there's a television crew in the lobby. Devon Gail apparently needs me to explain what a cookie competition is. This doesn't seem to be the time."

She ran her palms over her face. A wave of defeat washed over her, or perhaps it was the feeling of thick, greasy pancake makeup and dried egg. "Fine. You're staying here? Then we should sit down later. Because all I want for Christmas is a divorce."

Good, she thought as she turned on her heel. That would show him not to play games with her. What was he thinking, just showing up like that, sending her brain skittering in the middle of an important interview? Anna held her head up high as she headed out of the kitchen and through the swinging door. She stopped. Flossie was standing there, eyes wide. "What?" Anna said.

Flossie twirled her finger. "Turn around."

Anna did as told. Her heart plunged as she felt Flossie's fingers on her back and realized what she was doing. "Oh my God," she whispered.

"Yeah, that's right," Flossie mumbled. "Your mic was on."

Anna's throat tightened. If her mic was on, then her words had just been broadcast through the speakers in the lobby. "Thanks," she said meekly. There was a brief pause. "What did I say?"

"Oh, let's see." Flossie pulled up her hand and counted on her fingers. "Holly jolly bullshit, Marian can't clean or work a computer, Devon needs you to explain cookie competitions..." She frowned. "Did I get everything? Oh wait! You want a divorce for Christmas." She tilted her head and looked at Anna. "Do you want to slip out the back? I can run damage control. I'll just tell everyone you're on drugs."

Anna winced. "I don't think that would help, actually." She sucked a breath. "No. I'll go in there."

And so she trudged, one heavy step at a time, chin up and heart pounding, back into the lobby. When she stepped through the doorway, she forced a bright smile and slid her clammy hands down her ridiculous dress. "Sorry, everyone," she chirped. "So sorry about all that. Just a touch of domestic...bliss."

All movement in the room halted, and people avoided her eyes. Someone in the back coughed. Anna pressed her hands together. "I have some cookies in the breakfast room if anyone's interested? And I'll brew some fresh coffee. Or tea. You can have tea instead."

She was looking at Devon, who was scratching at the back of her neck with one slender index finger and staring at a spot on the floor. "Thanks, Anna," she said. "We have a long drive."

"Then you'll need something for the road," Anna said cheerily, and wrapped an arm around her shoulders. "Listen, I'm terrible at interviews, but I'm really good at hospitality. Bring Tom and the crew. And — Oh! Charis?" she called out over her shoulder. "I have plenty of hot chocolate for the kids. With whipped cream and marshmallows."

There, that oughta fix things. Joy to the world and deck the halls. *Fa-la-la-la-friggin'-la.*

CHAPTER TWO

THE INN WAS decorated. For some reason, Ben hadn't expected that. There were candles in the windows and garland on the banister, and there was even a giant fir tree in the two-story lobby, decorated with white lights and ribbons. As Flossie led him up the stairs to his room, Ben couldn't help but ask, "Did Anna hire someone to decorate?"

"No, she did everything. Charis and I helped, but it was mostly Anna." Flossie's eyes were amused. "That surprises you," she observed.

Ben lifted his shoulders and tried to look nonchalant. "I didn't think she cared for Christmas."

"She doesn't. But she does care about her business, and that would suffer if the inn wasn't decorated for the holidays."

Yeah, that sounded right. Ben lifted his duffel higher on his shoulder as they set foot on the second-story landing. He hadn't known what to expect when he'd first seen Anna, but he hadn't dwelled on the possibilities for too long. He was going to see her, and she was going to respond in some way, and then he would react, and so forth. It was the way of the world, and he didn't see how it would be productive to worry about it any which way. Never in a hundred years could he have predicted walking into a mess of cameras, or seeing Anna in a beautifully decorated inn, dressed as — what had she said? Santa's helper. But then again, pretty much everything was unpredictable when it came to him and Anna.

When he'd gotten the call from Flossie, he'd pulled his phone away from his ear to check the number again. "Let me get this straight," he'd said. "You want me to do a job?"

"Yes," had come her quick response.

"At the inn. The Archer Cove Inn."

"That's right. We have a hole in the roof of one of the guest cottages, and it needs to be fixed ASAP. Are you available?"

Ben had scratched at his cheeks as he'd thought about it. "Yeah, I'm available." He paused. "Does Anna know I'm coming?"

"Yes, absolutely. She told me to hire you."

"She did, huh?"

Something about that had lit hope of a reunion. He knew it was foolish to allow himself to go there, but there it was. For the last few days, it had been all he could think about. *Anna hired me. She wants to see me again.* The moment he'd seen her face — those narrowed eyes, those parted lips — he realized that Flossie had set him up. She'd set them both up. As he walked down the hall, he eyed her. "You know, I should be mad at you, Florence."

"Me? Whatever for?" Her eyes widened playfully. "And don't call me Florence, *Benjamin*. It's on my birth certificate, but it won't be on my tombstone."

"Are you playing matchmaker here? You told me that Anna hired me, and that was a lie."

"It's her money, isn't it? She told me to call a carpenter, so I called the only one I knew. And here we are."

Flossie turned the key to room number 234, facing the back. The old inn was large, with over forty guest rooms and two guest cottages. The rooms weren't spacious, but they were furnished comfortably, and the furniture was high quality. When he entered, Ben set his duffel bag on the floor so he could run his fingers along the post of the king-sized bed frame. Cherry. Behind him, Flossie said, "Do you like it?"

She had one hand on the brass doorknob, the other on the doorframe, like she might lock him in. "It's great, but I don't need a bed this size. It's just me."

She shifted her weight from one foot to the other. "Do you...want a different room? I can see what else is available. Anna locks up most of the rooms in the off-season, so we may need to dust —"

"No, it's fine." The last thing he wanted was to be a burden to anyone.

He pulled aside the sheer ivory curtains to reveal a set of French doors. Nice, Flossie had given him a view of the water. This time of year the ocean was gray, but no less beautiful. He looked at Flossie. "Thanks. This is great. Does your sister know that you gave me a room? I think she'd rather put me in the dungeon."

"Probably. But she won't care. And if she does, that's what she gets for not walking you up herself." Flossie grinned. "You know, it's nice to see you again. It's been too long."

"It's nice to see you too, Flossie." Whether it had been too long was up for debate. "How's law school going?"

She fluttered her lips and lifted her shoulders. "The third year is so boring. I didn't even have finals, just a bunch of papers."

"Are you living here? With Anna?"

"Nah, I still live closer to school. But I'm staying here and helping out until spring term starts."

"Maybe we can catch up and grab a drink."

"That sounds great." There was the sound of something crashing downstairs, and Flossie winced. "I should get down there. I don't want Anna freaking out."

Too late for that, Ben thought. "See you later. You can shut the door."

He shucked his jacket and set it to hang neatly in the small closet. Then he stepped out onto a balcony that was only large enough for one person to stand on. But he was alone, so he stood there and felt the cold December air rip into his sweater. Cold air made him feel alive.

The fireplace lit with a switch. He enjoyed the warmth as he considered whether he should bother unpacking.

He could leave. He had some friends he could call to fix that roof, and Anna didn't want him there. If he didn't know any better, he'd think she was even angry to see him.

Ben unzipped his duffel. Who was he kidding. He wasn't going anywhere. He was there to do a job, and he knew everything about this inn. He wasn't about to trust it to someone else.

When he finished unpacking, he kicked off his shoes and lay back in the bed, resting his head on the mountain of pillows. He'd woken early that morning to make the drive, and the fatigue was catching up with him. Plus, he'd rather be seared with hot irons than hang out in that crowd downstairs.

He turned over, and his gaze fell on a floral-print pillow edged with frilly fabric. It was set on the corner of an upholstered armchair beside the fireplace. He smiled, remembering how Anna had fussed over fabric samples for weeks and asked his opinion about pairings. He recalled telling her that he liked that fabric. He still liked it. He closed his eyes and fell asleep.

Charis believed in auras and the healing power of essential oils. She always smelled a little bit like patchouli. She was sweet and slow to anger, and Anna told herself that Charis wasn't the type to get in a twist about things like her sister blaspheming the holiday festival on live television. Even so, Anna had a moment of panic when

Charis called the next morning and said, "You've been avoiding me." Confrontation wasn't normally Charis's style.

Anna was standing in the kitchen, wiping down the fronts of the white cabinets. Breakfast had concluded and she had hours of work ahead of her, and she must have had a lapse when she'd answered the phone. She had been sending all calls to voicemail. "Avoiding is the wrong word," Anna said. "I've just been busy, and yesterday you had the foster kids, who were very well-behaved, by the way. Even that one little boy who was wearing my best crystal vase on his head like a helmet." Anna forced a laugh. "Little bugger."

"There's a cat video," Charis said softly. "I hope you haven't seen it."

Anna's shoulders slumped. "Yes. I've seen it."

The entire disaster of a news segment was circulating the Internet, and it had taken all of half a day for someone to lift choice pieces of the audio and pair it with a video of kittens in Santa hats who looked like they were singing. It was titled "Holly Jolly Bullshit," and last she'd checked, it had received over 100,000 views. "I don't know why they chose singing cats. It doesn't actually make any sense." Anna wasn't a cat person, herself. They made her break out in hives.

"Because it's the Internet," Charis said. "People love cat videos almost as much as they love humiliating others."

Anna had made the mistake of reading the comments that went along with the video. People had called her "a waste of skin" and "a grinch," and a few hoped that her business would shut down. There was an entire debate on one site concerning whether she was fat or merely overweight. One person said she'd be more attractive if she lost fifty pounds, and suggested she wire her mouth shut. *So helpful.* Anna had been feeling less than kind toward humanity over the last twenty-four hours. "It's all right. I can handle mean anonymous people."

She wiped down the counters in the kitchen, scooping crumbs into the palm of her hand. She'd been short-staffed ever since Marian had stormed out, mumbling something about slander. Fortunately she didn't have too many guests to care for. There was that nice couple, the Andersons, who were in from upstate New York and visiting their children in Spencer. And there were a few business travelers passing through town, staying for a night or two. And then of course there was Ben. How could she forget. But he had been making himself scarce, and she hadn't seen much of him, other than watching him leave and enter the inn. Aside from the cat video and the various jokes on late-night television, Anna considered the crisis manageable. "It will all blow over," she said. "Give them a week or so to find someone new to pick on."

"Hmmm," her sister said, sounding unconvinced. "It's just...did you mean all those things you said about the holidays? It made me feel so sad to hear you say that."

Anna felt a stab of guilt. Her younger sister had lots of reasons to be angry right then. Anna had walked off in the middle of an interview in which she'd said all kinds of bizarre things about a festival Charis had worked hard on and truly cared about. But instead, Charis was sad that Anna didn't love the holidays? Anna felt like a jerk. "No, I *love* the holidays. Deep down." She released a breath. "I mean, it's kind of complicated. And I think it's only because I end up hosting holiday get-togethers, and I put a lot of pressure on myself to make everything perfect."

There was a pause on the other end of the phone. "Do you still want to plan the festival? Because if you don't it's fine with me. Really. I don't want you to do anything that upsets you. Especially after everything that happened this year."

There was that familiar ache in her chest. She didn't want to talk about it. Anna tried to jolt her voice with energy. "With less than two weeks to go? No way. I told you I'd help, and I'm committed."

"That's a relief. I was just —"

Charis broke off as a fit of coughing struck. She attempted to speak several times, but struggled to catch her breath. As the coughing continued, Anna frowned. "Char? Are you okay?"

"It's just my asthma," she said, her voice raspy. "It's been bad lately."

"Do you have ginger on hand? If not, I can go to the store —"

"Thanks. Yes, I have some ginger. And I've cut dairy and I'm drinking water. It's just this cold weather."

She coughed again, and Anna felt helpless. Her knowledge of homeopathic remedies stopped at ginger, and she only knew about that because Charis swore it helped. "If there's anything I can do..."

"Thanks, Annie," she said, her voice returning to its usual warmth. "And look, don't worry about the cat video, or anything that happened. Everyone's going to forget about it within a few days."

Anna's throat tightened. Up to that point, she hadn't realized how much the entire incident had upset her. "Thanks," she whispered.

"Also, if Sandy Thane contacts you, don't even listen to her," Charis added quickly. "In fact, don't even pick up the phone."

A knot formed in Anna's stomach at the name of the chair of the Chamber of Commerce. "Sandy Thane?" she asked numbly. "What's going on?"

"Oh, she's upset about the news segment. I'm trying to smooth things over, though, and you have enough to worry about. You're still coming to the Chamber of Commerce meeting tonight, right? We're reviewing final plans for the festival."

Anna closed her eyes and groaned inwardly. She'd forgotten all about that meeting. "Remind me what time it is?"

"Seven thirty." Another cough, but this one was brief. "But listen, I'm going to make sure this festival is the best one ever. Mark my words: by the end of the Jingle Bell Dance, you're going to be feeling some holiday cheer!"

Anna's fingers tightened around the phone. "That's great. I'm sure you're right. Feel better, okay? Love you."

"Love you more."

As they disconnected the call, Anna ground her teeth together. She dropped the phone forcefully against the counter and let out a growl of frustration. Everything about the holidays sucked. This would teach her to try to be festive. "Damn it!" she whispered. So Sandy Thane was upset about the interview, was she? Well she could just stuff a candy cane sideways up her —

"Bad day?"

Anna spun in place to see Ben standing at the entrance to the kitchen. He was wearing khaki cargo pants and a blue plaid flannel shirt with the sleeves rolled to his elbows. Anna glanced downward. No shoes. He was walking around in gray wool socks as if he owned the place. "My day is just fine," she replied tightly.

"Didn't sound fine just then." He reached into the fruit bowl on the counter and helped himself to an apple. He then rubbed it on his sleeve and took a bite.

"Please, just make yourself at home." Anna ran her fingers through her hair and sighed. "You know, I serve breakfast between seven and nine. All guests are welcome."

"I'll have to get up earlier tomorrow, then," Ben said through a mouthful of apple. "Overslept this morning."

Anna leaned her back against the counter and crossed her arms across her chest. She had a mental checklist of all the items she needed to accomplish before three that afternoon: cleaning the guest rooms and bathrooms, mopping the kitchen floor, and running to the grocery store to pick up cheese and crackers for cocktail hour.

But right at that moment, Ben's presence was the most pressing item on her mind.

He wandered over to the stainless-steel refrigerator, opened the door, and stuck his head inside. "Do you have any orange juice?"

Anna studied him. "I'm afraid I'm all out."

"Eh. No problem. Cranberry's fine."

He emerged from behind the refrigerator door with a glass carafe filled halfway with red juice and closed the door with a socked foot. He set the carafe and apple down on the island and headed to a cabinet. "I'm just going to grab a glass," he said. It was sort of like asking permission, she supposed.

Anna felt a tension headache coming on. "Hey, uh, Ben? How long are you planning on staying here? It's just that this is a busy time of year for me."

He reached for a glass, firing a half-smirk over one broad shoulder. "That's Anna-ese, if I'm not mistaken. Translation: It's been great seeing you. Now get the hell out of Dodge. Am I right?"

She looked down at a speck of mud on the floor tiles, feeling transparently rude. "Look, I'm not charging you to stay here. And if Flossie hired you to fix the roof in the guest house, then I guess I'll honor the contract. But don't you think it's a little strange? We've been separated for months. You should be serving me with divorce papers."

"Because that's all you want for Christmas. Yes, I heard."

She'd thought about filing herself, but the process seemed overwhelming. They would need lawyers, and money, and there would be a division of assets. Frankly, the amount of paperwork seemed outrageous, considering how easy it was to get married. He walked back around the island to his breakfast and pulled a wooden stool from beneath the counter. "I can't serve you personally with divorce papers. It has to be done by a neutral party."

"So you've looked into this already."

"Nope. Just heard about it secondhand."

He grinned at her then. A genuine grin that crinkled the sides of his eyes and sent warmth coursing through her veins. Damn him for being so hot. She'd never been able to resist him.

Without a word, Anna retrieved a light-blue ceramic coffee mug and filled it. Then she slid it across the counter to him. "Here. I just brewed a fresh pot." She hesitated, wiping her hands on her apron. "Can I get you something else to eat? I can make you some eggs if you want, or some toast or a bagel." It was the polite thing to do. What kind of host would she be if she allowed her guest to eat only an apple for breakfast?

That smile again, and this time a scratch at his bearded cheeks. "Toast would be great."

She remembered that he liked sourdough, so she put two slices in the toaster before retrieving the butter from the refrigerator. "You still haven't answered my question," she said.

"I know." He bit into his apple, chewed, and then took a sip of coffee. "Good coffee. Do you have the paper?"

"In the lobby."

He shrugged. "Don't bother getting it. I'll pick it up later."

Anna's jaw tightened. She'd learned early on that Ben wasn't one to talk about anything until he was ready, and shame on her for being such a sucker for the strong silent types. He was perfectly content with questions and uncertainty. She could stand there and repeat herself over and over, and he would deflect until she cried from frustration and quit. Then he'd wonder what he could've said to upset her so much. It was maddening, really.

She set his toast on a yellow ceramic plate and slid it to him, along with the butter. "I hope you don't mind helping yourself. I have to mop the floors."

"You're short-staffed," he said easily as he lifted the butter knife. "If you need help, I'm not busy today."

Anna retrieved a bucket from the utility closet and filled it with hot water. "You're not fixing the roof?"

During a recent heavy rainfall, the roof of one of the guest cottages had sprung a leak. When Anna made her rounds to assess the damage, she'd found water pooled on the floors. The carpets were ruined, as was some of the furniture. That roof needed to be repaired before the next storm, or the damage could be significant.

"I've got some materials coming in later today. I'll begin work tomorrow. There's no rain or snow in the forecast this week, so it should be fine." He took a sip of his coffee.

Ben was a carpenter, but he was best known for woodworking. When they'd first met, she'd pored over a portfolio of his work, sighing over the smooth curves of dining room chairs he'd crafted, or the stair railings he'd painstakingly sculpted. His work was ornate and elegant — inspired. For that reason, he was in demand and basically nomadic, moving from job to job around the East Coast.

Anna wet the mop and pushed it across the tiles. There was something satisfying in cleaning, and when she rinsed the mop in the bucket and saw the clear water turn grimy, she realized the tile floor was in worse condition than she'd appreciated. Had Marian never mopped it at all? She felt her anxiety drop away as she continued, up, down, losing herself in the task so that she actually started when Ben cleared his throat and said, "You have some rotted boards on the back porch. If you're not going to put me to work inside, I'm going to fix them."

She dunked the mop into the bucket and wrung it out again. "You don't need to do that. You're a guest at the inn."

"We both know I'm much more than that."

He stood and emptied the remains of his breakfast into a trash bin. Then he rinsed his plate and set it in the dishwasher. She'd always appreciated that he'd been neat. He came up to her then, and his gaze was so intense that it sent her heart thundering. She could smell him, the scent of his soap and cologne, the faint smell of sawdust.

He always smelled like the wood he worked — how had she forgotten? And his breath was tinged with the bitter coffee he'd just drank.

"You don't want me here. I see that. I wouldn't have come if I'd known. But now that I'm here, we're stuck with the situation until I leave. We can either agree to make the best of it and maybe salvage what's left of our marriage, or you can continue pretending that what happened between us never happened at all."

Anna's lips parted. "Ben, I —"

"I don't believe in divorce, Anna. And God help me, but I'm going to somehow convince you that you don't believe in it, either."

His voice was soft, something in the tone almost sad. But he didn't explain himself before turning and leaving her alone.

CHAPTER THREE

THE FIRST TIME Ben had pulled into the Archer Cove Inn, the driveway had been gravel and riddled with holes. He clenched his teeth and gripped the wheel of his pickup truck as it bobbed to the right and left, and wondered whether his GPS had sent him in the wrong direction. But no, there it was: an old white Victorian inn, pocked with peeling paint and rotten wood. Birds were nesting in the gable trim, and one of the balusters on the front porch was broken in half, hanging like a loose tooth. A blonde woman dressed in a white puffer jacket was standing on the front steps, waiting for him. She was wearing one of those hats like his grandma used to knit. Fair something. Fair Isle. He realized later that the shade of blue matched the flecks in her eyes.

He pulled the truck in front of the porch and had barely set his foot on the ground when she came over. "You must be Benjamin?"

"Ben. No one calls me Benjamin unless I'm in trouble."

He grinned, but she missed the joke. *All business.* He could handle that. Hopefully she had the sense to go along with it. He reached into the truck for a clipboard and his tape measure. She was still behind him, still waiting. "I'll just be a minute," he said.

"Take your time." But she didn't move.

He pulled his head out of the truck and closed the door behind him. She held out her hand. "I'm Anna."

She was pretty. He'd guess five foot four or five, blonde hair past her shoulders, wide-set blue eyes. Not thin. She had a softness about her, and dimples in her cheeks. She smelled nice, like baby powder. "Pleasure to meet you, Anna." He shifted his clipboard and tape measure so he could shake her hand. "This must be the place."

"Uh huh." She folded her arms across her chest and glanced back at the structure proudly. "The owners passed away five years ago, and the heirs have been fighting ever since. I just bought it. Probably saved it from demolition. Come on, I'll show you around."

The entire structure suffered from neglect. They walked around the porch, which was probably a strong storm away from falling down completely. Ben noted the rotting boards and balusters, the shakes that fell apart when he touched them. There was termite damage on some of the lattice work. Hopefully it didn't extend further. The interior was a little better, but holes in the roof had caused some water damage and mold. He'd have to gut a few rooms, replace the staircase, remove the wood paneling...

"So, not too much to do." She smiled at him brightly, and he couldn't tell for a moment whether she was joking.

"You know this is a major job, right?" He had to set her expectations. "The inn hasn't been maintained, so I've got to go back and do decades worth of repairs if you want to bring this up to code." He had almost ten pages of notes, and lots of questions about what he'd find when he started work.

"Yeah, yeah. I know. I'm planning to sell my eggs to finance the job." She broke out into a small laugh. "I'm kidding, Ben."

So, she was warming up, then? She had a nice smile. Real nice, the way it crinkled the corners of her eyes. "You can never assume anything. I've heard all kinds of things. Creative financing."

"In all seriousness, I have the money. I received a historic preservation grant and took out a bank loan to get this place up and running. I called you because you're the best. I want this done the right way."

He set his pen into his clipboard and secured it under one arm. "You called the right guy. I live for stuff like this."

Her shoulders relaxed, and a relieved smile spread across her lips. "I'm so glad to hear you say that. I contacted other people, but they weren't interested in the job. They told me it was a teardown."

They were standing back where they started, out by his truck. The afternoon sun already sat low on the horizon. Anna patted the rail on the porch fondly, the way one might pat a loyal dog. "I just love the history of the place. I couldn't stand by and allow it to be torn down if there was anything I could do."

Ben reached out to touch the same rail. When he pulled back his fingers, they were flecked with paint chips. "We'll bring it back to life. All I need from you is a few days to run the estimate." She agreed.

He'd grown up in the area, only an hour away. Ben had realized after he left home that people in New England measured distance in travel time, while everyone else measured in miles. Maybe it was curious, but he thought it made sense. There were only twenty-four hours in the day — a person should know how much of his life it would eat up to get to the nearest convenience store. When he took the job at the inn, travel was a condition. Basically, he didn't want to do it. "If I'm going to come in on schedule, I can't travel an hour each way to my parents' house. I need to make the most of daylight."

"On schedule" meant he would be finished before Memorial Day and the start of the summer tourist season. It was going to be tight. "Fine, I'll give you a room," she said, just like he knew she would. Anything to get the job finished on time. All business.

She was living in the property, in one of the cottages. There was a path that led right from the kitchen to the cottage door. "It reminds me of growing up," Ben said. "My dad was a carpenter, and he built a shop for himself. He always liked living close to work."

They were in one of the guest rooms that day. She was shredding a carpet into squares, and he was pulling down wood paneling. He liked that Anna wasn't afraid to get dirty. She was out a lot, selecting paint and furniture, but Ben liked working most when they wound up in the same room. "What kind of carpentry?" she asked.

"Same kind as me. He started making these dining room tables a few years ago. He makes the top out of a single piece of wood. Just takes it lengthwise from the tree, makes a thirty-foot table. He's sold a bunch all over Europe."

"Wow." Anna paused to blow a lock of hair out of her face. "I'd love to see pictures of them some time." She resumed work. "My dad's a trial attorney. Retired. But he raised us to be cautious. A part of him would die right now if he saw me hacking away at an old carpet without a face mask and goggles. There could be, like, toxic mold or something."

Ben yanked a board off the wall. "He was a trial attorney? And he didn't make you go to law school?"

"Oh, he tried. But I could never. And then my sister Charis basically starts crying at any sign of confrontation, so she was out. My youngest sister Flossie is going to law school, though. One out of three."

"Flossie? Is that short for something?"

"Florence. My mom was supposed to have a boy, and they were going to name him Matthew after Dad, but then they had a girl, so..." She brought the razor down against the carpet with alarming force.

"So they pulled a name out of a hat, is that it?" Ben tossed a plank aside. "Opened up one of those name books? Or were they looking at a map of Italy at the time?"

"Something like that." Anna giggled. "By the way, if you ever meet her, she's kind of a loose cannon. Sometimes the only way to rein her in is to call her Florence. You can keep that in your back pocket." She winked. "Never know when you might need it."

"What does that mean, he doesn't believe in divorce? Like, the existence of it?" Flossie stuck a hand into the brown paper grocery bag and lifted a block of cheddar cheese. "Because it's a real thing. I can tell him all about it if you want."

Anna smiled at that. Ever since she'd started law school, Flossie had become an expert on every legal issue in the world practically overnight. She probably got it from their father. "I don't think that's necessary," Anna said. "But thanks anyway."

Outside the kitchen, on the back porch, they heard the whirring of a circular saw. Ben hadn't wasted any time getting down to work. "He's been out there for hours," Anna murmured. "I feel sort of bad about that."

"It's not that cold today. Maybe forty degrees," Flossie offered. "Plus, you didn't ask him to do that. Your legs look great in those jeans, by the way. If I didn't know any better, I'd think you were trying to get laid."

Anna glanced down at her jeans. They weren't new, and she hadn't given much consideration at all to her wardrobe that morning. Well, maybe a little. But she wasn't about to talk to her sister about it. "Your language," she said, her cheeks warming.

Flossie yanked a red knit cap from her head and ran her fingers hastily through her strawberry-blonde hair. It tumbled, thick and tousled, to the middle of her back. Anna winced as she flung her hat carelessly onto the counter and proceeded to unbutton her wool parka. "What, 'laid' is a bad word now?"

"You can't speak like that here. I'm running a business. And your boots are wet," she added. There would be puddles on the floors.

"Sorry. I'll clean it up." Flossie reached down to unzip her brown knee-high leather boots, still grinning. "I can't keep up with your puritan values. I'm teasing, you know. But you should get laid. I encourage it."

Anna's lips thinned. "I'm not a puritan."

She hesitated as she arranged the boxes of crackers neatly on the countertop, trying to come up with examples to prove the point. Okay, so she liked things orderly. Neat and safe. *Clean.* Still. "Liking things to be a certain way doesn't make me uptight."

"Uh huh." Flossie retrieved her hat and parka from the counter and hung them dutifully on the coatrack. "You want to live in a catalogue. That's cool. I'm not judging."

Anna bit her tongue. Her sister was thirteen years younger. Lucky thirteen. It was like it was her mission to test Anna's patience, and what did she know about life, anyway? What did anyone under thirty know about *anything*? Especially when that person looked like Flossie did: long-limbed and big-breasted, with a sweet round face like a cherub. Great hair, soft and thick. Life was kind to girls who looked like Flossie. She could go around tossing her wet clothes in nice places, trailing puddles on clean floors, commenting on legs and talking about people getting laid, and she would be forgiven. On a pretty girl, faults could be charming.

Flossie twisted her long hair and then secured it into a messy knot. "Stay off the Internet, by the way. Everyone seems to have an opinion on that news segment. And there's a cat video —"

"Yes, I know," Anna said through a clenched jaw. "It's landed me on Sandy Thane's radar. Charis says Sandy thinks I've become a distraction." Just saying the words got Anna's blood pressure rising. "I can't go into detail. I don't even have any."

Flossie frowned at that. "A distraction, huh?"

"I guess I'm not quite festive enough."

"Your presence at the Jingle Bell Dance will make angels cry. Like they did when you said 'holly jolly bull penis.'" She snorted. "That was my favorite moment ever, by the way."

"Hello? Can I come in?" a voice called from the back of the kitchen and a small face emerged from behind the kitchen door. "Hello," she repeated.

"Hello, Mrs. Marlowe," Anna gushed. "Come right in. What can I get for you?"

The door opened farther and Mrs. Marlowe shuffled inside. She was a small-framed, elegant woman with chin-length white hair. "I was wondering if I can trouble you for a cup of tea?" She folded her hands as if in prayer.

"Oh, of course. I'll put the kettle on right now. It'll just be a minute." Anna set the silver teakettle on the stove.

"Thank you," Mrs. Marlowe said as she pulled up a stool at the counter and took a seat. "This is so lovely. John and I are enjoying our stay."

"Do you live around here?" Flossie asked. "If so, you should come to the holiday festival. It's next weekend."

"You don't have to," Anna said quickly. "You probably have something better to do."

"Nonsense. It's going to be great," Flossie said. "We're decorating the town Christmas tree, singing Christmas carols down Main Street, and then coming back here to gorge on cookies. What could be better than that?"

Mrs. Marlowe's eyes lit up. "Oh, is this the holly jolly bullshit?"

Flossie made a noise like someone had just punched her in the gut. Anna looked down at the floor and wanted to die. "Yes, well. You see, those words were taken out of context —"

"Don't tell me that now," Mrs. Marlowe said with a playful wag of her finger. "I thought it was the perfect name for a holiday festival. But actually, we're Jewish. Do you have anything planned for Hanukkah?"

Anna chewed on her bottom lip. The festival was touted as a holiday celebration, but it did seem rather Christmas-centric, didn't it? She felt ashamed as Mrs. Marlowe's gray eyes searched hers. "We — not exactly," she said. "But we should have something for Hanukkah."

"A Hanukkah party of some kind. With Hanukkocktails," Flossie said as she folded the paper grocery bag and smoothed it into thirds.

Mrs. Marlowe lifted her shoulders sweetly. "If you do, let us know. We're visiting friends, but we could certainly make the time."

Anna lurched toward the teakettle as it whistled. "What kind of tea would you like, Mrs. Marlowe?"

"I have my own in the room. A cup of hot water would be great."

"I'll get you a carafe."

Mrs. Marlowe left a few minutes later, clutching a white carafe of hot water to her chest. Anna and Flossie exchanged a glance. "Hanukkocktails?" Anna said. "Really?"

"I thought it sounded like a great idea. Of course, you'd have to run it by Sandy Thane." Flossie winked.

Outside, the whirring of the circular saw stopped. Anna peeked out the window and caught a glimpse of Ben standing between two sawhorses, measuring a board. Her stomach prickled. Something about him, having him close by again, stirred up those old feelings, made her remember how electrifying his touch was. She had only shared half of Ben's statement with Flossie, who didn't know that Ben had resolved to somehow win her back.

51

The notion secretly thrilled her. And to think that she'd been over him just two days ago.

It was confusing, to say the least.

Flossie crept up beside her and said, "You still want those divorce papers under your Christmas tree?"

"Yes," Anna said quickly, dropping the edge of the curtain and turning away from the window again. "Ben and I...it was a whirlwind romance. Everything happened too quickly, and you know how those things can go." Anna's hands flew as she spoke, almost as if she were trying to grab the right words. "Hot and heavy, and over in a flash."

"Emphasis on 'hot and heavy,' am I right?"

Flossie lifted the curtain again, and Anna couldn't help but take another look. Now Ben was lifting the boards and setting them into an orderly pile. Her breath caught as she imagined the muscles below his shirt, felt the ripple of his chest pressed against her —

No. This was a bad place, and she was not going there. "Emphasis on 'over in a flash,'" she murmured, and this time, stepped away.

She had toilets to scrub and beds to make. Nooks and crannies to dust. "I'll be making the rounds," she called over her shoulder, feeling less breezy than she sounded. Yes, Ben stirred something, all right, and part of that something was an ache she couldn't ignore. But she'd learned the hard way that Ben was nomadic, and these days she was in the mood for something more permanent.

Ache or no, Anna was moving on.

CHAPTER FOUR

ANNA STARTED SCRUBBING toilets the day she turned fifteen. "You'll have to wear rubber gloves," her grandmother said as she handed her a plastic bucket and a brush. "Use the cart upstairs, in the closet. It has bleach."

A job was a job. So what if all the other girls in her class were spending the summer as nannies to families who lived up on the cliffs? Or working at hip retail shops in Great Barrington? Anna's grandmother, the head maid at the Archer Cove Inn, had filled her head with all sorts of ideas about tips from wealthy guests, and she could use tips. They bought things she needed, like a car and — eventually — college courses. She resigned herself to scrubbing away.

The rubber gloves sure came in handy, though, and for more than the bleach. Sometimes the guest rooms were downright gross, like that one time when she pulled the comforter off the bed and a purple rubber dildo flopped to the floor. Or that other time she found a dirty diaper, wide open, on a desk. She'd found handcuffs and silk scarves on the bedpost and simply worked around them, leaving them neatly in position for when their owners returned. Entering a room was like taking a glimpse inside someone's world: seeing their private lives, their desires, their halfhearted attempts to hide messes or their rigid tidiness. But for every dildo and diaper, Anna learned there were many more items of beauty in those rooms. The loved dolls and teddy bears children brought with them, or the family photograph the business traveler would set on the dresser.

Anna had once confided in Flossie that she secretly enjoyed stealing these glimpses into her guests. "I don't mean to snoop. It's just that I sometimes imagine what it's like to be them."

"You mean, to have your own family and an actual identity separate from your business?" Flossie had shaken her head. "You do more than admire other people's lives. You try to live their lives, Anna. And you can't."

Anna thought about that comment as she wheeled the cleaning cart down the hall. Live other people's lives? Whatever. She didn't understand that comment now, and she certainly hadn't understood it then. She had a life, even if her sister didn't fully appreciate what it was like to live in the place she worked.

She passed through the rooms quickly. Like everything, it had become routine. Change out the linens, replace the towels, fill the soap dispensers. Lather, rinse, repeat. Had she purposely saved Ben's room for last? Maybe. Possibly.

Yes. Yes, she had.

She stopped in front of it, her heart thumping and her palms clammy. She didn't have to clean it. He wasn't going to say anything if she didn't, but then again, where was the harm? What was she afraid of, anyway? That he'd be sprawled out in bed, waiting for her? Now there was a thought. Fortunately Anna had more self-control than to meditate on that one.

Anna knocked on the door and waited for an answer. When it didn't come, she entered Ben's room, her blasted heart still jumping around. The curtains were pulled tightly shut, so she tied them back to admit the light and then glanced around. He'd actually made his own bed and straightened his room. A folded sweater on the armchair was the only evidence that someone was staying there. She couldn't decide whether she'd managed to make Ben feel unwelcome or he was just trying to be a thoughtful guest.

She made a quick round of the room, dusting the woodwork and remaking the bed so that it was *just so*. She ran the vacuum over the carpet and scrubbed the bathroom until it shone. When she was finished, her heart had settled into its normal rhythm, and Anna breathed easier. Yes, it had been jarring to see Ben, but he was right in a way. They were both adults, and they would manage. They'd made a mistake in getting married, that was all. Oddly, she still felt a heaviness in her chest. It wasn't until she'd locked his room again that Anna realized that this was disappointment. She'd entered his room expecting to learn something about him, but Ben wasn't a guest who allowed himself to be known. Nothing about that should have surprised her.

As she returned the cart to the closet, Anna decided that life really should come with an instruction manual. Or maybe Anna would sit down one day and write one, call it "How to Live," or even "Hints for Not Royally Screwing Up Your Life." Chapter one would be called "Don't Marry a Stranger." And boy, did she have plenty to say about that topic. Chapter two would be called "Live Your Life in Service," because that was the only way she saw. Maybe Flossie was right, and Anna liked to live through other people. What was wrong with that? Didn't she enjoy a richer life experience when she saw the world through her guests' eyes? A life lived vicariously was a life of empathy, of creating happiness for other people. *And for me?*

Anna pushed the cart into the utility closet and scrubbed her hands clean. It was getting late, and she had a cocktail hour to prepare for.

At ten minutes to eight that evening, the group crammed into the meeting room at the Archer Cove Community Center was still waiting to begin the seven-thirty meeting. Anna and Charis stood off to the side of the room and took attendance of the members of the Chamber of Commerce, but everyone was there.

Everyone except Sandy Thane, the woman who had scheduled the meeting in the first place. But no one was about to leave, because leaving would win the ire of the chair. So they stood around and drank instant coffee out of Styrofoam cups and waited. By the time the back door opened and Sandy swept inside, riding a gust of frosty December air, she was twenty-seven minutes late. It wouldn't surprise Anna if Sandy had taken her leadership cues from great dictators. She knew how to make an entrance.

Sandy had a full head of golden hair that she feathered and styled into a sort of helmet. She had tiny eyes that disappeared when she genuinely smiled, which was not often. Sandy had perfected the art of smiling without her eyes. Anna's gut instinctively tightened as Sandy crossed the room to take her seat behind the long wooden table. If Sandy Thane's personality were a food item, she would be a prune: wrinkled, oddly greasy, and distressing in large doses.

"Oh goodness, I'm so sorry to keep everyone waiting." Sandy pulled her long black wool coat off and handed it to the vice-chairman, who dutifully hung it on the coatrack for her. "Thank you, John. We'll begin in a moment."

Charis normally favored comfortable clothing, like tunic sweaters, leggings, and bulky wool socks. She worked at the bookstore in the center of town, where she was often stocking shelves and lugging heavy boxes back and forth across the salesroom floor. Unless there was a special event, she almost never dressed up. That evening, however, she was wearing black slacks and a pink cashmere turtleneck sweater that clung to her thin frame. "We're the first item on the agenda," Charis whispered. She stuck her thumbnail in her mouth and chewed.

"Don't be nervous," Anna said. "We've gone over everything. It will be fine."

And it would be, Anna was certain. Because no matter how terrible that news segment had been, Anna and Charis had spent weeks developing sponsorship opportunities for the festival with local businesses, many of which were now invested in its success. This was larger than Anna and her big mouth, and even Sandy Thane understood that. The show had to go on. "It's not like she's going to call everything off," Anna said.

Charis turned her big blue eyes to Anna and shook her head. "You never know with Sandy. She may take over the entire thing."

Anna stopped herself from getting too excited about the idea. Really, as far as she was concerned, if Sandy wanted to take over the festival, she could have it. Anna was confident she could find a more enjoyable way to spend her many, many hours. But a takeover would be devastating to Charis, who loved planning the festival more than any human being should love planning anything. Anna was trying to understand.

She reached over and gently pried Charis's hand from her mouth before giving her a squeeze. "We're okay. I'll do the talking." She was the one who had the explaining to do.

"All right," Sandy's voice boomed from the front of the room. "Now let's see, what's the first item on the agenda?" Anna raised her eyes heavenward as the chair lifted a slip of paper and squinted at it as if she didn't know exactly what it said. "Ah, yes. The holiday festival. Is Charis here?" She was looking right at her.

"Yes, ma'am." Charis took a step forward.

Sandy shuffled some papers around in front of her. "And Anna, of course. Lest we forget."

Anna sucked a breath at the dig. Then she held it for a few beats so that she wouldn't end up snapping back. "Hello, Sandy."

She responded with a cold smile. "Hello, Anna. Let me be the first to say that you certainly made a splash with yesterday's promotional activities."

"Ha!" The nervous laugh burst from Anna's throat. She pressed her lips together tightly before adding, "I know what you're thinking, but it's managed to drum up a lot of attention for the event. In marketing, the worst sin is obscurity, am I right?"

Judging by the lift of Sandy's right eyebrow, Anna was not, in fact, right. "I have received several calls from concerned parents who wonder whether this year's festivities are taking on a more, shall we say, PG-13 tone."

Anna's face pulled, her tight smile mirroring Sandy's. "We're doing the same thing we do every year. But you already know that, so you should've had no problem answering those questions."

She felt a childish flash of triumph as Sandy blinked her eyes in surprise, but the chair recovered her composure quickly. "I couldn't be sure. Not when a co-chair's language is so plainly in the gutter." She folded her hands on the table and leaned forward. "So what you're telling me is that there will be no unpleasant surprises from here on out? No vulgar interviews and foul language? I mean, my goodness. It's a Christmas festival. There will be children there, and who knows how many of them were tuned in to the news yesterday to hear you talk about bull genitalia."

"Oh, for God's sake. Now that's enough." Anna set her hands on her hips. "I made a mistake, okay? It happens. I have stage fright, and my ex-husband walked in just as we were starting the interview, and I had no idea he was coming. My sister invited him."

"I didn't," Charis added softly, then folded her hands demurely before her.

"Right. It was Flossie, not Charis," Anna agreed.

"Ex-husband?" The bespectacled vice-chair tilted his head with interest. "I thought you wanted a divorce for Christmas?"

His question was followed by a string of agreeing murmurs and someone at the other end of the table saying, "I thought the same thing."

"I think it came as a revelation to many of us that you were even married," Sandy said pointedly.

So, what — now her marital status was a topic of interest for the Chamber of Commerce? Charis started coughing.

Anna stuffed her hands into her pockets and glanced down at the floor, trying to summon the remains of her patience. "We're basically divorced. It's just a technicality... Look, I don't really think that matters. All that matters is that I'm really sorry about what I said, and for the record, I friggin' love the holidays. I love the crap out of Christmas, okay? Oh, but Sandy? It's not really a Christmas festival. It shouldn't be, anyway. Because not everyone celebrates Christmas. So I want to clarify that."

This nabbed Sandy's interest. "What do you mean? Are you planning new activities? I thought it was the usual Christmas festival."

Anna glanced over at Charis, but she was staring at her feet and chewing on her lower lip. "No, we don't have any new activities planned for this year. It's just a suggestion for future years, that's all. To be more inclusive."

Sandy laughed drily and sat back in her seat. "Well, let me be blunt: I highly doubt that either of you will be planning this event next year or in any future year. But thank you for the suggestion."

Anna's hands hurt from clenching her fists so tightly, and she couldn't bear to bring herself to look at Charis. She only hoped she wasn't crying.

"We have the schedule for the festival here," Sandy said. "Does anyone have a question about anything else? If not, we'll move on to item two on the agenda." When no one on the board replied, she looked at Charis and Anna and said flatly, "I guess you're dismissed."

Anna turned and grabbed her coat from a chair in the back of the room, Charis close behind her. "She's a monster!" Anna growled as she and Charis stepped outside and into the chilly evening. "So basically she only called us in there so she could chew me out?"

A light snow was falling, and a dusting covered the sidewalk as the two women crossed to the parking lot. Charis coughed as the cold air hit her lungs. "I guess so," she said once she'd caught her breath. Her hands were tucked deep into her coat pockets, and her gaze was directed at the ground.

The lights on Anna's red Toyota Corolla blinked as they approached. Anna unzipped her coat. After that meeting, she was boiling. "How dare she, you know? Who does she think she is? After all we've done for this stinking festival. And you've done this for years, and it's always been great!"

She couldn't decide what made her angrier: the indignity of being hauled in front of the entire board to explain her unfortunate word choice, or the injustice of hearing that Charis was being held responsible for her mistake. Sweet Charis, who wilted under criticism. It would probably take her a solid year of intense meditation and yoga to even begin to come to terms with what had just happened. Was there enough lavender essential oil in the world to calm her? As they climbed into the car, Anna fastened her seatbelt and stole a glance at her sister. "I'm going to fix this, Char. I promise."

And she would. She was the older sister, the responsible one. She didn't know exactly how she'd manage to turn this around, but... "It's Christmas, right? The season of miracles?"

Charis broke into another coughing fit, and Anna turned up the heat. They were heading back to the inn, where Charis had left her car. "First thing I'm going to do is make you some tea," Anna said. "I don't have ginger, but chamomile is good, right? And I have some local honey. We'll sit in front of the fireplace and we'll figure this out. And we're not talking about Sandy Thane. Not a word. Starting now."

Charis was quiet. Too quiet. Her soft, almost white blonde hair was down, and it framed her face in thin ribbons. She stared straight ahead at the road as it slipped beneath the car, her mittened hands resting on her lap. Anna clenched and unclenched the steering wheel and concerned herself with plotting revenge. She'd never been the type to egg a person's car, but until just then she'd never had a reason, either.

They headed into the inn and hung their coats in the closet. Anna didn't have to ask Charis to remove her boots. She did so automatically and lined them up neatly on the mat beside the door. As Anna entered the lobby, she was surprised to see a fire already blazing and Ben and Flossie chatting on the couches. "Hey, look who's back!" Flossie beamed and held up a glass of wine. "Perfect timing. We just opened the bottle."

Anna sucked a breath. Whose side was her sister on, anyway? "We sort of had a rough night."

Ben lifted his glass to Anna and Charis. "Even more reason to join us." He patted the cushion beside him and moved over, grinning when Anna elected to sit on the couch beside Flossie instead. "Fair enough," he said cheerfully, and took a sip of wine.

Anna couldn't bring herself to look at him, to chance her hormones going into overdrive. *Good Times Ben.* It was how she secretly thought of him when he was like that, all charming and funny. The man could turn it on, that was for sure. He was wearing a dark sweater that hugged his muscles very nicely, and jeans that would probably make her lose her train of thought if she saw his bottom. Clearly he'd set his charm on high, too, the way he was shooting her that sexy smile. Damn, he was playing dirty.

Flossie had her red hair pulled back in a long braid and flung over one shoulder. Her smile faded when she saw her sisters' glum expressions. "What happened to you two? Was it that Chamber of Commerce meeting?"

Anna puffed out a breath and leaned back against the cushion. Her entire body ached, and to think that she had to wake up the next morning and do it all again. She really should go to bed, but the fire felt so warm and inviting. "We're not talking about it, actually."

"Sandy Thane is a nitwit."

The comment burst from Charis, who was sitting alone in the recliner, her fists clenched in her lap. Flossie, Ben, and Anna stared at her, slack-jawed. "What?" Charis said. "You all know it's true."

"Yeah, but you're not the one we'd thought would say it," Flossie said, and rose to her feet. "I'm getting you a glass of wine. Let's see what else you'll say."

Anna pulled a blue throw pillow into her lap and tucked her feet beneath her. "I don't want you to worry about it. I'll take care of things with Sandy —"

"No. There's no fixing anything with her." She turned her gaze to Anna, resolute. "The only option is to scorch the earth."

Anna turned at the sound of Ben's startled laughter. "Are you going to burn someone's house down? Because if so, I'm going to turn in for the night —"

"We're not burning anything except bridges," Charis said with a spooky calmness. "If this is the last holiday festival I'm ever going to plan, then I want to give Sandy a reason to remove me. I want to make this the worst festival Archer Cove has ever seen."

Her eyes were bright blue, shining with something that scared the crap out of Anna, who laughed nervously and shot a glance at Ben. "Hey now, no need to do that. Everyone loves that festival, and we sort of, you know. Have to live here."

Jeez, it felt a little bit like trying to turn the Titanic around. Something had shifted in Charis, and Anna realized that her sweet-natured, asthmatic little sister wasn't as delicate as she'd always assumed. The change was a bit fascinating, in a train-wreck sort of way. "I can't stop thinking about what she said, about whether the festival was taking on a more adult tone. How ridiculous is that? I've planned this thing for years, and it's always been the same, and I've done everything Sandy has told me to do." Charis shook her head and narrowed her eyes.

"I'm going to ruin it. I am. I don't even care. We'll put the X-rated in Xmas, by God."

Hoo boy.

Anna leaned forward to pat Charis's knee. "You do care. You care a whole ton, and I'm not going to let you ruin anything. In fact, I think we should double down and make this the best damn festival the town has ever seen. You know what I'm thinking? An ice skating rink on the back lawn of the inn. A snow sculpture contest."

"Hanukkocktails," Flossie suggested as she handed Anna and Charis each a glass of red wine. "For our Jewish friends."

"Yes, Hanukkocktails," Anna nodded sagely. "Ben, you can help us with that, since you're half Jewish."

"Mazel tov," he said.

"In fact, screw Sandy and her Christmas festival. We'll make this the best winter holiday festival anyone has ever seen."

"You could add fireworks for Chinese New Year," Ben suggested with a shrug. "It's a little early, but cultural authenticity doesn't seem to be the plan if you're serving cocktails for Hanukkah."

"I don't see why we can't serve latkes," Flossie said. "I mean, we can nod to tradition. Plus, they're delicious."

"So we have fireworks and latkes, good. What can we do for the solstice?" Anna glanced around the circle and saw only blank faces. "No one knows anything about the solstice? That's fine. We'll table that for now."

A smile spread across Charis's face — not an evil smile, either. "We should light the Yule log for our Pagan friends."

"There will be something for everyone," Anna declared. "It will be inclusive, and amazing, and Sandy Thane will lose her damn mind when she sees it."

"I love it," Charis said, and lifted her glass. "To the best interfaith Christmas festival ever."

Flossie, Ben, and Anna raised their glasses. "To being everything to everyone, or at least most things to most people." Anna smiled. "Cheers."

CHAPTER FIVE

THE FIREPLACE EXTENDED straight through the lobby to the second story. It was built of stones collected from the property and the surrounding area. Rocks were as plentiful as sand, and old stone animal pens were numerous in the wooded areas of Archer Cove, dating back to a time when the whole place had been farmland. Anna loved those stone walls, and she loved that fireplace. "I don't want you to touch it," she told Ben the first time she'd brought him around. "Maybe add a mantel. For stockings."

"Stockings?" Ben grinned. She was adorable, and she wasn't even trying. "Okay, I won't touch it. Promise." He wasn't a mason, anyway. He'd have no reason to do anything with the massive stone structure. Even so, he thought of that conversation every time they sat in the lobby and had one of their renovation meetings. Anna called it a tête-a-tête.

"Tête-a-tête time!" Anna pulled him by the sleeve. "Take a pillow," she said, directing him to one of the throw pillows on the floor.

"Assume the position," he said, with mock boredom. "I know the drill."

She had her hair pulled back in a long braid, but pieces of it fell out around her face. She giggled sweetly and sat beside him, pulling a giant book of fabric samples into her lap. "I need your advice. Today we're considering guest cottage number one."

"You realize I'm billing you for this, right?" He leaned back on his hands, hoping she'd move in a little closer. He was delighted when she did.

"Hey, last time I checked, I'm providing you with free room and board for like, months here."

"Free room, at least. I bring the boards."

"Oh my gosh, you're *so* funny, Ben. Tell me, is it extra for the bad puns?" She rolled her eyes and shifted a little closer to set part of the book on his lap. "Now, focus. I'm looking at these, with the thin gold stripes. I need to decide between blue, red, and green."

He frowned at the fabric samples, but he couldn't concentrate. Their thighs were touching, and she was warm and she smelled so pretty. "What's this for again?"

"Guest cottage number one."

"Upholstery?"

Based on her sigh, you would've thought he'd said something completely off-topic. Like she'd shown him the fabric book, and he'd said, "Oh, are you designing a ball gown?"

"Ben. Focus." She put her two fingers in a "V" and brought them to her eyes. "Look at me. We chose the upholstery fabric two weeks ago, remember? This is for the throw pillows."

"Ah, of course. How could I forget?"

She held his stare for a few moments before turning shyly away and glancing back down at the book on their laps. "This is important. Life-changing."

"Yes."

He couldn't take it anymore. He reached up to touch her, just to brush that little piece of hair back behind her ear. She sucked a breath and turned her gaze slowly, looking up at him through her long black eyelashes. "You have to pay attention," she whispered.

"Oh, I will. But not to that."

He closed the book and set it on the floor. Then he knelt beside her and cradled her cheek in his hand. He kissed her softly on the lips. "Anna. You don't even realize what you do to me."

Every morning, he looked forward to seeing her. His pulse accelerated at the sound of her footsteps. She'd started entering his dreams. It had gotten to the point where he thought he might be losing his mind.

"Oh, I think I do," she sighed, and reached for his shirt to pull him closer. "I think I do."

They had sex right there in the middle of the lobby. Urgent but sweet at the same time. His knees were bruised later from the hardwood floors. After it was over, Ben was still kneeling, buttoning his shirt. "I'm sorry," he said, because he didn't know what else to say. She was a client.

"I'm not." She slipped her sweater over her head and smiled. "I thought it was nice."

He exhaled. "Me too."

She invited him to stay with her that night, and the next one, and the one after that. One afternoon while he was working, she brought out a battered shoebox and presented it as if she were sharing her diary. "I can't believe this is still here."

"What's that?"

He stepped off the ladder as she hurried over to his side and tore the top from the box. "My collection."

Inside the box was a pile of junk: old coins and backs of earrings, gold chains and plastic toys. A mother-of-pearl pendant. "You collect garbage," he murmured, hoping he was wrong.

"No," she beamed, her eyes shining. "I collect forgotten things. I started this when I was fifteen. Guests would leave things around, so I would keep them safe in case they ever called. Look — I even found a wedding band once." She held up a man's gold band. "I can't believe the owners kept this for all those years."

"You're a collector of the forgotten."

"I never understood how people could lose precious things and forget about them," she mused as she lifted a necklace that sparkled with glass emerald studs. "Even this. It's not the nicest thing in the world, but it must've meant something to someone."

As he folded his arms across his chest and admired her, his heart flooded with warmth. She was a sweet, sensitive woman. "You're sentimental. I like it."

She set the lid back on the box and gave a halfhearted shrug. "I take it you're not?"

"I've never thought about it. I've lost things before, but I haven't called. Losing things...it's just life." Did she honestly think that guests should be calling her about costume jewelry? Or was she thoughtful enough to want to help them just in case they did?

"Well, for some people, I guess." The side of her mouth quirked upward. "But tell me: what about a wedding band? Would you call about that?"

"Oh, now *that*." He chuckled and stepped back onto the ladder. "If I ever found someone I cared about enough to marry, yeah. I'd come back for the wedding band."

"Good," she said, and tucked the box beneath one arm. "Then you're still welcome in my bed tonight."

\#

Ben tossed and turned all night, his mind racing. Red wine always did that to him. It must be something about the sugars. At four in the morning he sat up in bed, set his feet on the floor, and wondered if he'd ever learn his lesson. Probably not.

He took a hot shower in the white claw-footed tub and skipped the shave. The beard was a new development, but he liked it. Maybe it was his imagination, but it seemed warmer, too. A cold front had moved in yesterday. He'd actually felt the temperature plummet while he was working outside, repairing the boards on the porch. The day would be bitterly cold, and he'd be outside repairing a roof. Better to keep the beard.

His mind kept wandering to places it shouldn't go. Like to that one night when they'd been standing in the lobby and talking about wainscoting, of all damn things, and she looked at him and he knew that she wanted him to kiss her. So he did. He stepped in and brushed her hair gently off her shoulders, and he leaned down and kissed her. She moaned against him and he nearly lost control right then. Good thing it all happened quickly, in a flutter of clothing and hot, bare skin. He was all set to take her right there, right on the Persian rug, when she'd sighed into his ear and said, "The couch."

"What?" He could barely hear her above the pounding of blood in his ears and his labored breath.

"Over here." She took him by the hand and led him to the brand-new white couch. Then she'd climbed on top, turning and leaning her chest against the back pillows, her back to him. "I want it like this," she said.

Good lord, was she the hottest woman ever. He thought of that now as he headed into the kitchen and prepared a pot of coffee. Even the innkeeper wasn't up yet, he mused, and he already had coffee and blue balls.

"Ben?" He turned as Anna stepped through the swinging door, looking fresh-faced despite the garish hour. "Is something wrong?"

And that's when he realized that everything was wrong. Somewhere along the way, his life had gone off the rails, and he needed desperately to get back on track. If only he could figure out how to reach her.

But all he said was, "I made some coffee. I'll get you a cup."

It was strange, having Ben here in her kitchen again, pouring coffee for her. She had a flash of déjà vu as he handed her the mug and she caught that sexy, straight-out-of-bed smile. Like he had some thoughts, but they were all dirty as sin. A chill passed over her and she accepted the coffee, grateful for a distraction. "That was nice of you," she said, her breath darting over the steam rising from the mug. "Thanks."

"I shouldn't have had that wine last night." He leaned his back against the counter, looking deliciously tousled even though he smelled clean. "Kept me up all night." He darted a glance at her. "I should've come to see you."

She nearly choked on her coffee but managed to merely dribble it down her chin. Classy. Ben chuckled and handed her a dishtowel. "Sorry. Didn't expect that."

"Yeah, me neither," Anna said as she patted at the front of her sweater. "Jeez, Ben. You're full of surprises, aren't you?"

His stare was startling in its intensity. "It's like torture for me, being here with you again, and not able to touch you. I lose my head sometimes."

Anna looked away. Gosh, didn't she know it. She'd lived in that inn for years. Every day, she worked there. How had she managed to stay focused for so long, to not think of him each and every time she took a step? Memories of Ben were all over the place — sweet torture, as she recalled their time together. Their many, many times together.

A flush crept up her neck, and Anna turned away. The coffee was too hot. She needed to cool down. A glass of cold water should do the trick. "Ben. It's over between us. I can't rehash old arguments. We tried and it didn't work out. There's nothing more to it than that."

He kept his focus on her, clearly unconvinced. "We've said that before. Then we end up in the same place again."

"And it's exhausting." Anna filled a glass with water and held it in her hands. "My life is here. In this inn. You're traveling."

"So?"

"So I need someone to be here with me, not in North Carolina one week and Maine the next." She took a sip of the cool water. "I'm sorry Flossie brought you here. I'm not sure what she told you, but it wasn't the truth."

His eyes searched her and he lowered his voice, stepping closer. "She said there hasn't been anyone else for you since you told me to leave."

God bless it, did her little sister have loose lips. Anna's cheeks heated again. "That's true. We are still married, and I took those vows seriously, even if we did get married under...trying circumstances."

He winced as if she'd struck him. "Trying circumstances, huh? I married you because I love you."

Anna felt the tug of his words, and she didn't want to slide down that slope just then. There were other things to focus on: the festival, her guests. Herself. Maybe they'd loved each other, but it wasn't enough. "People can be in love and still not be right for each other." Her throat squeezed. "I will always care about you, Ben. But please respect what I'm saying."

She set her glass on the counter and walked to a drawer to retrieve an apron. If breakfast was going to be served on time, she'd better get baking. Ben stood in place, seeming lost. "You know I respect you. But I want you to know that I still love you. I need you to understand that."

If Anna stayed in that kitchen one minute longer, she feared she would start crying. She opened the refrigerator door to retrieve eggs, cream, and cheese, pretending she couldn't find the ingredients just to have a moment to collect herself. The things Ben did to her, the expectations and demands. He loved her, did he? But he'd spent so much time away. That wasn't love to her, and this was where they were incompatible.

"The discussion is closed," she said, her arms loaded with food, as she closed the refrigerator door with her foot.

But Ben had already slipped out of the room, taking his coffee with him.

#

There was an expiration date on their love affair, and they both knew it from the beginning. Maybe that was careless of Anna, to leave her heart exposed so thoughtlessly. But during the months that she and Ben were together, everything was the way it should have been. She felt beautiful. Ben had a warmth that she couldn't resist even if she'd wanted to. Their nights together were dizzying and their days together were busy but pleasant, and when it was over, there were no sobs or dramatic good-byes. They knew it had to end.

She was raking the front lawn one October afternoon when she heard the truck approach — this time on crushed shell, not gravel. Anna glanced up, expecting to see a guest. Her heart stopped when she saw the man climb out of the vehicle, a bouquet of pink roses in his hand. He smiled that gorgeous smile that had made her go all weak nearly a year earlier and said, "Hello, beautiful."

"Oh my gosh!"

She actually threw the rake to the ground and ran to him like she was some lovesick teenager. It seemed right, though, to throw her arms around his neck and kiss him right there. Then she stepped back to look at him, her eyes not believing. "Ben. I didn't know you were coming back." She stroked his cheek with a gloved hand, leaving a smear of dirt.

"Are you surprised?" He said it with a hopeful twinge, like that was the only thing in the world he wanted.

"Completely." She laughed and struggled to breathe. "Come in!"

He was only in town for a few days, visiting his folks because his mom had a fall. He told her all of this in the kitchen, which was the only place in the house where guests usually didn't venture. They couldn't keep their hands off each other. She looped her fingers behind his leather belt, he rested his hands in the back pockets of her jeans. "I missed you," she said. Her lips came up high enough to kiss his chin, which was just a little prickly.

He groaned and pulled her hips closer to his. "I missed you too, sweetheart."

They fell right back into bed like no time had passed at all. When he left, there were no tears or good-byes. It was just how things were. Ben moved from job to job, and Anna stayed in one place. But that first stretch of time was the longest they were ever apart. From then on, it was understood that Ben would return. And right before their lives changed forever — nearly two years after they'd first met — they took a walk on Arrow Beach.

They were bundled in jackets to keep out the chill, and they walked side by side with their fingers interlaced. He stopped short on the pier and turned to Anna, his nose pink. "You know what? I love you, Anna Tumblesby."

It was as if he'd just come to that realization. It was what she loved about Ben, that he was willing to say whatever popped into his head. He was fearless. There was a surge in her heart because, see, she believed him. He left and came back and left and came back, and she thought the coming back part was the most important. She figured the coming back part said "love." "I love you too, Ben Tanner."

He stayed for two weeks and took a job in Florida for eight, then one in Georgia, and he was back. Then he was gone again. Anna kept busy with her inn and didn't think about it. By that point, they loved each other, and she told herself it was enough to weather any storm. Hadn't she learned that in fairy tales?

But she'd since come to understand that love wasn't constant and unyielding. It was more like a season: shifting and changing shape and form. The love she and Ben shared wasn't any different. It wasn't forged in steel. It was a winter promise that melted in the heat of spring.

CHAPTER SIX

ANNA DIDN'T MAKE it over to Hedda's Bakery until late the next morning. She'd found it was the best time to visit the little bakery, anyway. There was a lull in their business between breakfast and lunch — the last remaining lull, since the business was rarely slow anymore.

"Good morning, Hank," she said to the man behind the counter. "Nice to see you."

"Anna. What a pleasant surprise."

Hank Mallory reminded her of a television sitcom dad, with salt-and-pepper gray hair and classically handsome features. He was wearing a blue apron and seemed to be writing something on a pad, but he set it aside as she approached. "I'm working on a new menu," he explained. "I get tired of baking the same thing day after day. Time to mix it up a little."

"I can understand that." Anna rotated her breakfast menu constantly so that she was never baking the same dish in any two-week period. "It keeps things interesting."

"Funny you use that word," he said, leaning one elbow against the pastry display. "Because I saw your email about the holiday festival. You're planning a Hanukkah party now?"

"That's right. It's just going to be a cocktail party at the inn. We'll light the menorah, spin a dreidel. You know."

"Uh huh." Hank's eyebrows pulled closer together. "Just so I understand: you want us to cater the event. With latkes."

"Correct. And any other Hanukkah-related dishes you think would be appropriate."

"Appropriate to serve with cocktails."

"Hanukkocktails. Yes."

Hank scratched gently at his temple. "You've given me a lot to think about here, Anna."

"Oh, great!" She clapped her hands together. "I know that whatever you come up with will be perfect."

Hank reached for the pad and pen, still frowning. "Challah something, maybe. Challah bread pudding?"

"That sounds wonderful," Anna said over her shoulder as she headed into the kitchen. "I'm clearly in good hands. I have to go upstairs to see Jessie. Mind if I take the back way?"

Hank waved a hand at her and wrote something down. Anna couldn't help but smile as she breezed through the simple white and stainless-steel industrial kitchen and out the back door. She'd been working with Hedda's Bakery for years, and Hank had never steered her wrong. As far as she was concerned, she didn't need to do any more planning for the Hanukkah party.

She headed up the back staircase to Jessie Mallory's chocolate shop. The entry was shielded by a pink-and-white polka dot awning, and the glass door read "Sweet Possibilities" in white swirling letters. Anna opened the door and heard a bell chime, followed by a wave of warm air. Jessie came bouncing out of the back room, her light-blonde hair pulled into a tight ponytail, her eyes shining. "Hi Anna! Are you here for the truffles?"

Anna had been ordering truffles for turndown service for over a year now — since back before Jessie had even opened her shop. "I'll take them if they're ready."

"They're ready. It will just be a minute." She lifted a hand and ducked into the back room.

The shop was converted from the apartment where Jessie, her uncle Hank, and her cousin Wren used to live. The space was cozy, with a few glass displays loaded with shiny chocolate treats, fudge, and a few gummy items. In a side room, Jessie had shelves lined with candy in plastic bags and little pink boxes: wrapped caramels, foil-wrapped chocolates, rock candy, assorted old-fashioned penny candies, and assorted chocolate gift boxes. This time of year, most of the candy was holiday-themed, with foil-wrapped trees, Santas, and snowmen. Jessie had strung festive white lights around the shop and hung fresh evergreen wreaths tied with red velvet bows.

"Here you go," Jessie announced as she reemerged, carrying a large cardboard box. "This should get you through the next few weeks, at least."

"Super." Anna accepted the heavy box and then set it down on the counter. "Did you get my email, by any chance?"

"I did, but maybe you can clarify things for me," Jessie said tactfully. "I'm not familiar with solstice chocolates."

Anna had spent some time the previous evening researching solstice celebrations, but she was at a loss as to how to incorporate the traditions into the holiday festival. When in doubt, choose chocolate.

Anna reached into her pocket and found a tube of lip gloss. Her lips were feeling chapped from the cold. "We're expanding the offerings at the holiday festival this year," she explained. "Recognizing diversity and so forth to make a truly inclusive winter celebration. I want to recognize the solstice, but I don't exactly know how to include that."

"So you want me to come up with chocolates?" Jessie lifted an eyebrow.

"Chocolate bars, maybe? With a decorative wrapper? Maybe Santa can hand them out to the kids."

"Hmm." Jessie pressed her lips together thoughtfully. "This is really last-minute, but I'll see what I can do."

"I appreciate that. I know that whatever you come up with will be great."

Jessie didn't look so convinced as she tilted her head to one side, a semi-smile crossing her face. "You may want to lower your expectations there. The best I could probably do is wrap some chocolate bars in decorative paper."

"Perfect!" Anna swept the gloss over her lips. "Done deal. Between you and me, this is more about sending a message to Sandy Thane that Charis and I are not her lapdogs."

"Oh, I see," Jessie said, in a tone that suggested complete confusion. "Is this about that news segment? I don't get what the big deal was. I had no idea you were married, by the way."

Anna forced a chuckle and waved a hand. "It was a whirlwind. Just a couple of crazy kids making a huge mistake."

"Ah. I've been down that road myself." Jessie looked down and away. "I'll tell Nate you stopped by. He was here a little while ago. He'll be sorry he missed you."

Nate Lancaster was Jessie's boyfriend, and the two were adorable. Anna found it endlessly amusing that Nate, a personal trainer with a body like Adonis, was dating Jessie, a sweetheart with a chocolate shop. She couldn't think of two people she'd rather see together. "I'm so sorry I missed him. Yes, please send him my regards." Anna hefted the cardboard box filled with truffles off the counter.

The door behind her chimed and a blast of cold air hit the back of Anna's legs. She turned to see Jessie's cousin, Wren, who was grinning from ear to ear. "Hey, Jess! And Anna — so nice to see you." She came over and gave Anna a quick kiss on the cheek almost as an afterthought. She was clearly there to see Jessie.

"Hey." Jessie beamed and brushed her hands down the front of her apron. "I didn't know you were coming by."

Wren shook her head. "How could I not stop in? I'm so happy!" She ran behind the counter and gave Jessie a big hug and a kiss on the top of her head. "How are you feeling?"

"Tired, but okay." Jessie glanced over at Anna. "Sorry, Anna. Let me ring everything up for you."

Anna felt her smile freeze on her face. "No, no. Just send me the bill, it's fine." She shifted the box in her arms. It was awkward. "Everything okay? Have you been...under the weather?"

She shouldn't have asked, but she'd never been one to leave well enough alone. And she thought she knew the answer already. Her heart pounded as the cousins exchanged a secretive glance. Jessie lifted her shoulders and said, "I'm expecting."

"Ah." The breath flew out of Anna's lungs. She set the box down on the counter and reminded herself to breathe, then she tried again. "How wonderful!"

"Isn't it?" Wren rubbed her cousin's back. "Jess called to tell me a few days ago. I've been out of town. I couldn't wait to get back!"

"Thanks." Jessie looked shyly at her feet. "It's totally unexpected. Nate and I have only been dating for a few months —"

"But you've been friends for a *long* time," Wren said. "It's a solid foundation."

"There's so much to think about. There's the shop, and Nate just opened his gym —"

"Hey, don't get overwhelmed yet. We're all going to help you out."

Anna's face hurt from smiling. She rubbed at her cheeks, hoping she didn't look too awkward or obvious. "Wow. That's wonderful news, Jessie." She paused. "So you're...how far along?"

"About thirteen weeks. My pants are tighter, but no one else seems to notice yet." Jessie's hand flew to her abdomen, which was concealed by a pink-and-white polka-dotted apron. "But the baby looks healthy, and I'm grateful I'm finally past the nausea."

Anna bit her lower lip and scooped the box back into her arms. "If wedding bells are in the air, you let me know. You can use the inn. Not that you need to get married, of course." She shook her head. "Sorry, that sounded old-fashioned of me —"

Fortunately, Jessie didn't seem offended. "Actually, we've talked about it. Maybe a little ceremony with our families and closest friends. We could never see ourselves having a big wedding, anyway." She smiled. "Thanks."

"You're welcome." Anna hefted the box and started to turn. Then she remembered her manners. "This is such wonderful news, Jessie. You and Nate will be fantastic parents." Her words sounded mechanical to her own ears.

"Thank you, Anna."

"And thanks again for the chocolates. My guests love them."

"Of course." Jessie smiled and gave a little wave. "Good to see you. Stay warm out there."

Anna made her way down the back steps. She decided not to take the short cut through Hedda's and instead walked around the building to her Corolla. She popped the trunk, stowed the chocolates inside, and walked quickly to the driver's seat. She fastened her seatbelt, put her key in the ignition, and placed both hands on the steering wheel. Then she sat for a moment, perfectly still, before bursting into tears.

It had been just over a year since Anna had gone to the doctor complaining of flu-like symptoms and come out pregnant. Not by the doctor, of course. Oh no. She knew who the daddy was, and he was in South Carolina at the time.

Pregnant. The news turned her bones to jelly. Pregnant, with an inn to run all by herself. She was still hobbling around after recovering from a broken ankle. She held herself together as best she could that day, but when she finally went home, she locked the door behind her and sobbed.

"You're sure?" Ben said after a long pause on the phone.

"Yeah, positive. I had the test done at the doctor's office. They drew blood to confirm it."

There was another long pause, and Anna felt the panic set in. She was responsible for another human being, but she had no say over whether Ben would step up. Would he stay far away? Would they end up in court, fighting about who was responsible for braces...or even paternity? "If you're thinking it's not yours, let me assure you —"

"I know," he said quickly. "I know it's mine. I just wish I wasn't so far away right now." She heard him draw a breath. "How are you feeling?"

Anna hadn't expected the question. "N-not great. I thought I had the flu. I ache all over, and the nausea is bad." She was crying as the reality began to settle. "What am I going to do?"

Ben finished the job early and came back to Archer Cove three days later. They went for a walk around the inn property, and he dropped to one knee in the gardens, by the fountain. It was frozen over. "Marry me," he said as he pulled a black velvet box from his coat pocket.

Anna nearly fell over. "You don't want that."

Yes, those had been her first words. She should've said "yes," she knew, but all she could think about was that she and the baby were going to tie Ben down and change his life forever. Did he need the marital ball and chain to go with that? "I'll only hold you back," she explained. Her happy-ever-after moment, and she was trying to convince her Prince Charming to run.

A shadow crossed Ben's face, a quick flash of pain. "Anna. I wouldn't ask you if I didn't want this."

And so she'd said "yes," and allowed him to slip a lovely solitaire ring on her finger, but it still felt like trickery. She could raise a child on her own if that was the hand she was dealt. She didn't need Ben to love her out of obligation. She didn't want that.

They married two weeks later in front of their immediate family members. The next day, Anna was back to work. Charis urged her sister to take a honeymoon. "It's December. No one expects the inn to be open. This is the perfect time to take a trip somewhere."

"Maybe," had been Anna's response, but she didn't mean it. If they went anywhere, it couldn't possibly be romantic. Not with Anna'a nausea and fatigue. A few days off? She'd be snoring by sunset.

Ben was a good sport, at least. He declined some new jobs to be with her. At her first doctor's appointment, he held her hand as the doctor pressed a wand over her belly, searching for the heartbeat. "It's still early," the doctor said. "You're twelve weeks along?"

"About."

Anna stared up at the fluorescent lights on the ceiling and told herself to breathe. They would figure something out. Maybe they'd have to sell the inn, or move to a less expensive region of the country, but Ben seemed like he was committed, so really —

Ben squeezed her hand as they heard it. *Tap tap tap tap*, in quick-fire succession. Their baby's heartbeat. Anna's own heart swelled. "Is that it?" she choked.

The doctor smiled. "That's it. One little heartbeat."

Anna and Ben looked at each other, both too overcome with emotion to speak. And for the first time since she'd received the news, Anna thought that maybe everything would be just fine.

"You know what this means, don't you?" Ben said. "We're having a baby. Which means that we're going to need a nursery and a crib. I'm going to build it."

They were in Anna's little cottage, which they were going to outgrow in no time flat. She had two small bedrooms, a tiny kitchen, and a living space. Like everything else in their lives, they were going to have to figure it all out. "I love that you want to build a crib, but do you think we have the room?"

"We'll clean out your office and I'll customize it for the space." He said it so matter-of-factly, like there was nothing he would rather do than work around that issue. "I've already thought about it. I know exactly what I want to do."

It was January by then, and Ben was taking small jobs in the area. He used his parents' woodshop to work on baby furniture. Anna came home one evening to find a white crib in the room they had started to refer to as the nursery. She gasped when she saw it. Ben stood by, his chest out slightly. "Do you like it?"

It was painted white, with gently arching curves on the matching end boards. Anna set her hand on her heart. "Ben. I love it. It's so beautiful."

"Of course it's beautiful. It's for our baby."

Our baby. Anna loved him so much at that moment that she couldn't even speak. All she could do was to reach out and hold him, and know that he wasn't going to leave her.

*

The diagnosis was Trisomy 13. Their baby had a third number 13 chromosome. There was no warning or hint of a problem until she'd gone for the first ultrasound. "It's random," the doctor assured them gently. "It's nothing you did or could have prevented."

Anna was numb at the news. Their baby could be born unable to see or hear — assuming she made it to birth. She'd be lucky to see her first birthday. *She*. Because in the series of tests that had followed that ultrasound, they'd also learned the gender.

Ben sat beside her in the examining room, his eyes on the cold gray floor tiles, his hands limp on his lap. The doctor was telling them they had the option of terminating the pregnancy, but all Anna could think about was how desperately she wanted her baby to live, even if it was against all odds. "I can't do that," she whispered.

"It's a lot to think about," the doctor said, his voice warm with compassion that made no practical difference in anything. "Go home and think about it."

Anna didn't think about termination, though. She didn't think about the diagnosis, even. Everything had suddenly been taken from her. All of her happy endings and fairy tales, her belief in life's problems working out for the best. Her baby, and the plans she'd made for their future life together. All of it, gone. She put her hand on her swelling belly and imagined the life stirring, and she knew that she loved her child. "I'm so sorry I didn't realize it until now," she whispered.

Ben was quieter. Absent. He took another job and worked late. They didn't talk about it because there wasn't anything either of them could say. They'd solved a lot of problems together, but this wasn't one of them.

Then, at eighteen weeks, the doctor broke the news. Their baby's beautiful heart had stopped beating.

There was no funeral, no baby to hold and grieve. No death certificate or gravesite or public acknowledgment that their child had ever existed. She was given the choice to deliver the baby or to have it removed through a surgical procedure, and she thought her heart would cleft in half right then. Anna opted for the D&E, and just like that, she was no longer pregnant. She left the hospital empty-handed, and when she came home, she went into the nursery. The crib was gone, replaced by her office furniture. It was a signal that life was supposed to return to normal.

She hadn't told many people about the pregnancy because they had learned of the trisomy early. Some who knew assured her that there was a reason for everything. Sandy Thane was one who somehow knew. "It was God's will," she said. "He must have needed another angel."

Anna bristled at the suggestion that God would take her child. If she'd ever been a person of faith, she'd fully lost her faith by then. But when Sandy had patted her on the shoulder and said, "You're young. You have plenty of time to have more children," Anna really wanted to punch her in her horse mouth.

"No one saw her as a person except us," she said to Ben one evening, the raw hurt apparent in her voice. "Everyone else wants to pretend she never happened. It's easier for them that way." But even Ben had grown quiet. He didn't want to talk about the baby, either.

Ben left two weeks later. He took a job in Delaware that was supposed to be three weeks, but stretched into five. On the evening he called to let Anna know that he was heading to Upstate New York for a few weeks, she told him to not bother coming back. All of her illusions had evaporated, and she finally saw the marriage for the fiction it was. Their child had brought them together, but now there was no need to pretend anymore.

"It's over, Ben," she said.

Her chance at a family and a life full of happiness. Her innocence. There was no turning back the clock. It was all just...over.

CHAPTER SEVEN

FLOSSIE WANTED TO make herself useful while she was staying at the inn, so Anna sent her on errands and assigned simple tasks, like arranging breakfast Danish and the scones for afternoon tea service. It was only as a last resort that Anna decided that Flossie needed to learn how to make the housekeeping rounds. With the planning underway for the holiday festival, she was simply running out of hours in the day.

"You have to fold the flat sheet back like this and then tuck it in," Anna said as she demonstrated. "The fold should be approximately six inches. And don't roll your eyes at me. I'm trying to teach you how to do things the right way."

Flossie folded her arms over her chest and sighed. "I know how to make a bed."

Oh, she did, did she? Then why was her room a disaster every time Anna went in there? Anna bit her tongue. "I know. I'm only trying to help."

Five days to Christmas, and they would be busy through the weekend. Flossie might not have been good at housekeeping, but she was turning out to be darn good at advertising, and the inn was going to be busier than she'd ever seen it at that time of year — all thanks to the festival. Ben and some of his friends in the area were constructing a skating rink on the back lawn, complete with a small booth that would serve hot chocolate. Snow wasn't in the forecast for the weekend, so that was a problem for the snow sculpture competition. Fortunately Flossie had found a place that agreed to rent a snow machine for the day. That would be set up on the side lawn.

For Anna, it was all a matter of being careful what she wished for. A popular festival and a busy inn — she wasn't totally sure how she was going to manage it all. Flossie would help, of course, and Charis had even taken a few days off work at the bookstore to pitch in. If she got desperate, she supposed she could lean on Ben. She was hoping not to get that desperate.

If things with Ben had been strained before, the situation hadn't improved. Anna couldn't exactly ignore him when he was working on the festival with her. He'd done a great job on the roof of the guest house, and she appreciated that, but he'd been making himself scarce for the most part. Busy working, or scarce, and when he wasn't either, he and Flossie were chatting it up. If Anna had been the paranoid type, it might have bugged her. Big time.

She dropped a pillow into a newly laundered pillowcase. "You and Ben have been catching up a lot."

"Hmm? Oh, yeah. We've had some talks."

Flossie tucked a cream-colored blanket beneath the mattress, and Anna held her breath because the blanket was short on her side. Not saying a word. She set the pillow back and reached for the other one. "Some talks? About what?"

Subtle she was not, and Flossie arched a brow at her. "I'd tell you, but then I'd have to kill you."

"Hilarious. Fine, I don't even care. Don't tell me." Anna slipped the pillow into a new case, pausing for a beat before saying, "Seriously, what are you talking about?"

There was something going on, she just knew it. They would sit off in the corner with a cup of coffee and lean in together, serious looks on their faces. Flossie and Ben had always had a rapport, and Anna found it sweet. He thought of her as a kid sister, and she knew that Flossie thought the world of him. But this was too much. Blood before water and whatnot. Ben was the ex (sort of), and Flossie was in his corner. No fair.

But Flossie wasn't about to divulge. "We're talking about my changing body. He has some great insights into what to do when I have that not-so-fresh-feeling. You wouldn't think so, just by looking at him." She smiled sweetly.

Anna rolled her eyes. "Uh huh. Does he tell you where he goes?"

"Where he goes? What do you mean?"

NATALIE CHARLES

"When he leaves the inn for hours at a time. Is he working a job or something?"

"I dunno. He's your husband. You should ask." She walked over to Anna's side of the bed to adjust the blanket. "Crap. I did this wrong."

"It's not as easy as it looks. Here, let me show you how I do it." Flossie stepped back as Anna untucked the blanket and repositioned it on the mattress. "You do this enough times, you start to develop a method. You don't have to use mine, but you'll get the hang of it soon enough."

She expertly tucked the blanket, creasing the corners just so to keep it from bunching. The guests would slip beneath her handiwork that evening and feel as though they were wrapped in a snug cocoon. Anna swept her hands together once she had finished. "There. You'll try the next room, okay?"

"Sounds good." Flossie shook her head. "I don't know how you do it, Annie."

"Do what?"

"All of this. You're running this inn by yourself. You basically have demanding house guests like, all the time. You cook for them and clean up after them and pretend they aren't being disgusting when they complain that the light fixtures are too low for them to use the reverse cowboy position in bed."

Yes, that had happened recently. It was one of those times that Anna had wished for brain bleach. "It's my job to make people feel welcome, that's all."

"Sometimes I think you take on too much," Flossie said quietly. "You have these perfectionist tendencies, and it's like you can't accept weakness."

The blood rushed to Anna's neck as she realized the conversation had taken a sudden turn. "Is this what you and Ben talk about, my perfectionist tendencies? I mean, besides your menstrual cycle, of course."

Like he was one to talk, when he was so precise with his carpentry and woodworking. Since when was taking pride in one's work a bad thing?

But Flossie was unrattled as she pulled the comforter in place. "Not exactly. But we did agree that you're too hard on yourself, and that you have a hard time asking for help." She paused to look her sister in the eyes. "You pushed him away, Annie. He loves you."

"Yes, so I've heard." So now he had Flossie acting as the messenger? What was next, a choir of angels? She shoved the decorative pillows in place, her eyes stinging and her chest heavy. "Let's get this straight: what happened between me and Ben is none of your business. You've meddled enough."

It was harsh, but goodness. Anna and Ben had their reasons for the separation, and Flossie didn't understand the first thing about it. Anna drew a breath and attempted to channel her inner Zen. She wasn't the Zenful type, but guilt over hurting her little sister's feelings accomplished something similar. "I shouldn't have snapped at you. I'm sorry."

Flossie bent down to pick up something on the rug. "Looks like someone dropped a pearl earring."

Anna set her hands on her hips. Always with the change of subject, that one. "Set it on the nightstand. Did you hear me, Flossie?"

"Yeah, yeah. I won't meddle. You're sorry for snapping. Don't worry about it." She carefully placed the earring beside the ceramic lamp. "People must lose things here all the time. Half your job must be mailing things back."

Anna's thoughts flew to her little shoebox of lost treasures. "You'd be surprised. People lose things and forget about them."

"Even jewelry?"

"Jewelry, photos. I even have a wedding band that someone left years ago."

Flossie's eyes widened. "What? You'd think that if something was that valuable, someone would never forget it. I can't imagine." She paused, and Anna could see her mind working rapidly. "There's gotta be some illicit reason behind that wedding band, don't you think? Something juicy?"

Anna thought of her own wedding band and engagement ring, which she'd placed in a small white box and tucked away in her underwear drawer. "Sometimes things don't work out. It's not always juicy." She lifted the pile of dirty sheets and headed for the door. "Come on. We have a few more rooms to do before we prepare for afternoon tea and coffee."

*

A bracing wind brushed against his neck as Ben set the level on top of the board. *Finally level.* The structure for the ice skating rink was finished, and with barely any time to spare. He heard a crunch of boots on the frozen grass behind him and turned to see Anna heading over with a thin stainless-steel thermos in her hand. "I just made some mulled cider. I brought you some. I mean, I was making some for the guests," she added, apparently not wanting him to think he was too special.

"And I'm a guest, even if I'm working off my room charges." Ben smiled and accepted the thermos gratefully. He was freezing out there. "Thanks. What do you think? We're finally ready to fill the rink."

It wasn't a huge rink, or impressive. Just some boards and a lining, but it would do the trick. "At least it's cold enough. If we fill it now, it will be ready by Friday. Nothing but freezing in the forecast."

Anna was fully bundled in a black knit hat, a thick matching scarf, and a white puffer jacket. Her skin was so fair that her cheeks and the tip of her nose were already bright pink. Her blue eyes were shining as she said, "It reminds me of something out of a Norman Rockwell painting."

"You mean old-fashioned?" He chuckled and poured himself some cider. It was steaming hot. "It's the simple things in life, right? Like sharing mulled cider with a beautiful woman beside an empty ice skating rink."

Her eyes crinkled, her smile half-concealed behind her scarf. "I think that's one of his classics."

"And don't worry about the lawn, either. I had to rip out some grass to get the ground level, but I'll reseed in the spring." How hopeful of him, he thought, to assume he'd be invited back to reseed. "It will be as good as before."

"That's good to know, because Charis runs her Saturday morning yoga sessions here in the summer. It would mess with her energy if she had to relocate." She gestured to the cup in his hand. "Try it. I made it a little differently this time."

"Mmm." Ben took a sip of the drink and felt his insides begin to thaw. "This is great. It's like you read my mind. But you were always good at that, knowing what people need."

She looked down at her boots as if she were embarrassed by the compliment. "It's part of the gig when you work in hospitality. If I wasn't good at it, I wouldn't be in business very long."

"You're good at selling yourself short, too." He took another sip. "Empathy is a gift. You've got it, that's all."

He knew that empathy was both a sword and a salve. Anna could hurt as easily as she could soothe, and all because she seemed to innately understand what made other people tick. Like, for instance, the day she'd told him to never come back. Or right then, when she'd brought him cider. Sword and salve. It was powerful stuff.

She folded her arms across her chest, hugging herself as another arctic breeze swept in from off the Atlantic. "I still think of her sometimes. Do you?"

101

See, right there. She'd ripped a hole straight through his chest with a few carefully chosen words. Ben sucked a breath, but the pain remained. "Yeah. I do."

Of course he thought about his daughter. Their daughter. What might have been. Usually he couldn't, because the ache was unbearable.

"This should've been her first Christmas."

"Anna." He paused before he told her to stop, but he didn't know what this was all about, all of this dwelling on things that couldn't change. Ben gritted his jaw and said softly, "I know."

He knew. He *did*. He knew her heart was broken, and his was too. He knew that life was unfair and that people were oblivious to what they'd been through. He just didn't see how talking about it was going to change anything.

They stood there, side by side, for a while. He was staring at the whitecaps on the water, and wondering why the sky was always gray in December. No wonder everyone strung up lights at this time of year. The sun wouldn't come back until March.

"I'm glad you're here." She said it slowly, as if each word required great effort. "We have a history, and it's a little strange, but at least you understand. I get tired of pretending that everything's normal, and that this holiday is the same as the last one. Nothing's the same. Forever."

He glanced at her quickly from the corner of his eye and wondered how she wanted him to respond. He wasn't like her, knowing what to say and how to act. He often felt like he never got any of that stuff right. He settled on reaching over to gently pry her folded arms loose so he could hold her mittened hand. She let him. He squeezed her fingers. "Happy anniversary," he whispered.

She swallowed, and her bottom lip trembled. "Yes," she said.

CHAPTER EIGHT

THE HANUKKOCKTAIL PARTY was in the room where Anna served breakfast each morning: a room with two walls of windows that normally overlooked a stretch of lawn and the ocean. That evening, Anna kept the lights dim to allow guests a better view of the stars. A fire was blazing in the stone fireplace, and tables were set with white linens and candles. On the fireplace mantel sat a menorah lit with five candles. Anna had to admit it was even better than she had hoped.

"This is lovely," Mrs. Marlowe gushed, pulling her husband in tow. "I'm so glad we made the trip."

"I'm thrilled to see you again, Mr. and Mrs. Marlowe," Anna said as she gently touched Mrs. Marlowe's thin shoulder. "The Hanukkocktail Party is our kickoff event to the weekend festivities. Please, help yourself to some latkes and doughnuts, and we have specialty drinks at the bar."

They headed to the buffet table as more guests streamed inside the room. The turnout was astonishing, really, and the party had only just started. "Not bad, eh?" Anna said to Charis as she shuffled by with a tray of cinnamon sparkle martinis.

"Sandy has called me five times this week. I've sent her to voicemail each time, and I refuse to listen to the messages." Charis grinned. "We've gone rogue. This is a new thing for me."

"But you have to admit, it's working out all right," Anna said. "This is lovely, right?"

"Lovely," Charis agreed. "The perfect start to the best holiday festival ever."

The next day was Friday, but schools would close early for the holiday break. The ice skating rink would open at noon, and Anna would have hot chocolate, cider, and cookies for anyone who stopped by. The snow sculpture competition would begin in the afternoon, followed by the tree-lighting ceremony. Saturday would be more ice skating followed by the Jingle Bell Dance, caroling, and sleigh rides through the town. Anna felt exhausted by all of the planning she'd done over the past nearly two weeks, but now that the festival had arrived, she felt a surge of energy. And something else. Something that felt like holiday cheer, if she didn't know any better.

Flossie bounced over to her sisters with a big grin. "Hey, look over there," she said, pointing to two men talking in the corner. "A pastor and a rabbi walk into a cocktail party."

"What's the punchline?" Charis said.

"No punchline. I just love that this is a diverse crowd. It's actually working — isn't that nice?" Flossie ran her fingers through her long hair. "I'm going to get a drink. Be back in a few." She waved at someone across the room before bouncing off again.

It was working, thought Anna. Those words were music to her ears.

"Nice job, Anna."

She started at the man's voice behind her and spun to see Ben dressed in a blue Oxford shirt, a navy tie, and gray pants. His beard was trimmed and his hair was combed and he looked better than the beignets. "Thanks," Anna said. Then she realized she was raking him over with her eyes, and blushed. "Happy Hanukkah. It's nice of you to come."

"I wouldn't miss it. This festival is all I've been doing for the past week." He smiled as he said it, and stuffed his hands in his pockets.

He wasn't even exaggerating. He'd built the skating rink and the hot chocolate booth, and taken care of who knew how many other little details. "Yes, well. You know I'll compensate you for your troubles." Somehow. Money was tight, but it seemed only fair.

Ben chuckled at the suggestion. "And you know that I won't accept payment. Not in money form, anyway."

Anna blinked. "Money form? What's that mean?"

He stepped closer, coming up to her until she felt his warm breath bouncing off her face. He smelled like mint, and possibly cinnamon. "I'd like to take you out after this. Let me show you a good time."

"Oh." Anna looked down, her face on fire. "I couldn't. I have to clean up —"

"Nope. I already spoke to Charis and Flossie. They're going to handle everything."

But they won't do it exactly right, Anna wanted to explain. They might put the dishes in the wrong place, or forget to sweep the floor, and what if the liquor was left out? What then?

"Ben, it's not —"

"Anna." He squared himself so that he was facing her and then reached out a hand to touch hers lightly, as though he were catching a butterfly. "I fixed the roof on the guest house, didn't I? And I fixed the rotted boards on the porch."

She hesitated. "Yes."

"And I built you a skating rink? And a concession stand?"

"Yes."

"All I'm asking for is the privilege of having dinner with you. Do you think you could make the time? An hour or two, tops. You can't deny me. Not on Hanukkah."

Anna sighed. Maybe she was being unreasonable. Besides, she could come back later and take some time to double-check to make sure everything was in its proper place. No harm. "Okay. But I'll have to be back —"

"Yeah, I know," he said, laughing softly. "You have to be back home before your coach turns into a pumpkin."

His hand was large and rough, his fingers strong. But he held her hand so gently as he brought her fingers to his lips and kissed them. "We'll leave in an hour."

"An hour?" It was a quarter past six, and the party had just started. "I couldn't leave my own party."

Anna felt an arm across her back as Charis pulled up beside her and said, "It's not your party. It's my party, too. I'll cover." She glanced back and forth between Ben and Anna with a smile. "Go. Have dinner with your husband. It's long overdue."

Between the two of them looking at her expectantly...Anna resigned herself to defeat. "A girl's gotta eat, I guess."

"That's the spirit," Ben laughed.

Charis patted her on the back. "You're such a hopeless romantic, Annie. Try not to enjoy yourself too much."

At precisely seven fifteen, Ben pulled Anna aside and told her it was time to leave the Hanukkocktail party. "I have reservations," he explained, helping her into her coat.

Reservations? That sounded fancy, and suspiciously like a date. "Am I dressed all right?" She was wearing a black dress that fell to her knees. Simple, but elegant enough.

"You look beautiful," he said.

It wasn't until they pulled up to The Barn that Anna realized he had completely avoided her question. She wasn't dressed appropriately at all. Proper attire for dinner at The Barn would've been ripped jeans, a skintight sweater, and a push-up bra. "You're taking me to The Barn?" She groaned and slumped into the passenger seat of the pickup truck.

Ben seemed tickled by the whole thing. "Come on," he said as he unfastened his seatbelt. "They have great wings and fifty beers on tap."

Oh goodness.

Anna finger-combed her hair back and glanced down at her high heels. "I'm going to stand out. I can't go here. People will think I'm stuck up."

"Who cares what people think? Go snag your pantyhose on something if it makes you feel better. Mess up your hair a little. I promise, no one's going to be looking at you. It's karaoke night."

"Even better," she grumbled, and grudgingly exited the vehicle.

It was fine, she told herself as they crossed the frozen gravel parking lot and entered the tavern. Things happened for a reason, and the reason that Ben was taking her to The Barn was to show her that they were so obviously mismatched. Was this his idea of a good time, a noisy dive? She'd take a cup of tea by the fireplace and a good book any night of the year. If there was a silver lining, it was that she had only committed herself to an hour or two. She could handle it, and truth be told, the space was actually kind of...cute. For a converted barn.

The old, wide floorboards were polished, and the interior was divided between floor level and loft, with a bar in the far end. Waitstaff bustled between the simple wooden tables. And sure enough, space had been cleared out along one wall for a makeshift stage and a karaoke machine.

Ben held Anna's hand, leading her to the hostess stand (a hostess stand? At The Barn? She never would've guessed!). "Hello," he said. "I have a reservation. It's under Tanner."

Anna pressed her hand to her face. So he hadn't been kidding about that part. Fortunately, the hostess didn't look at them strangely. "Of course," she said, and pulled out two menus. "Follow me."

As they wove through the tables toward the far wall, Anna wondered if maybe she'd misjudged the place. She liked the white lights strung around the rafters and the giant evergreen wreath hanging near the entrance. When they arrived at a small table in the corner, the hostess took her coat and Ben pulled out her chair. "I'm not sure what to make of all this," she confessed. "I always thought The Barn was a dive bar."

"It's been under new ownership for the past two years," Ben explained as he took a seat. "They've kept some of the old touches. The antique bar, of course. Karaoke Thursdays. But the food is much better, and so is the atmosphere." He angled his head. "You've really never been here?"

She suddenly felt foolish. "Like I said, I thought it was a dive bar. And I don't get out much," she added. "Not with the inn."

"I'm glad you could get out tonight."

They shared a brief smile before Anna noticed the roses on the table. "These are beautiful. I sure didn't expect roses here."

"You like them? They're yours."

Anna leaned forward to smell one. Heavenly. "What?" she said.

Ben lifted his water glass, clinking ice. "They're special for this table. The reservations, remember? I know you think I brought you to a dive bar, but I'm actually trying to show you a good time."

"Oh. Well. Thank you, Ben."

Anna sat back in her seat as someone stumbled up to the microphone and started singing "I Will Survive." He was hopelessly off-key and had obviously been drinking. After two lines, Anna broke into a fit of giggles. "Oh my gosh. I don't remember the last time I was in a karaoke bar."

She looked to Ben, but he was snapping his fingers and bobbing his head, his face dead-panned at the tuneless crooner. Anna clamped a hand across her mouth and snorted. "Stop! Oh my gosh." Her ribs were starting to hurt.

"I appreciate the finer things, Anna," Ben said gravely. "Sorry if you can't dig this funky beat."

Funky beat? The singer was missing notes right and left, and Ben was practically dancing in his seat. She was

111

going to pee her cocktail dress if it continued much longer. But as the song ended and the audience applauded, she wiped the tears from her eyes and wondered when she'd last laughed so hard. It felt great.

Ben gave the singer a standing ovation and a few whistles. "Brilliant," he said as he sat down again. "It's not every night you see that."

"No." She giggled. "It's definitely not. I hope he has someone to drive him home."

"I'm sure his manager will take care of him. Guy like that? He has people." Ben reached for his water, his eyes playful. "I hope you're not enjoying yourself, Anna. Because that's not the point of this dinner. I'd really prefer if you take this evening seriously."

"Yes, sir. No problem." She fired off a salute.

"Good. Because I'm a man with very specific taste. I like my women stone-faced and uptight, and I'm seeing this new side of you right now. I gotta be honest" — he held up his palms in a sign of surrender — "it's kind of hot. You're throwing me off my game."

Anna grinned and set her napkin in her lap. She was liking herself just then, too. And she was starting to remember what she'd seen in Ben in the first place. "Sorry. I'll do my best to frown more."

"Please see that you do. It's Christmastime. No one should be happy."

Anna was no food critic. She enjoyed haute cuisine, but she wouldn't turn up her nose at a burger and fries. Good thing, because The Barn was still a burger-and-fries kind of place, and both were delicious. She polished off most of her meal and didn't feel a bit guilty about it. But when Ben asked to see a dessert menu, she groaned and said, "I'm stuffed."

"Nonsense. There's always room for dessert." He turned to the waitress. "We'll see two menus, please."

"Ugh." She set a hand over her stomach and shook her head. "I'm not even kidding."

"Neither am I. I'll carry you out if I need to. I'll put you right over my shoulder like a caveman."

They were sharing a bottle of white wine. Ben reached forward then and filled her glass. "Cheers, darling."

Darling. Her chest still warmed when he called her that, and she couldn't help but be proud to be with him. He was handsome, of course, but also charming and considerate of the waitstaff. A gentleman. *My husband.* Anna took a sip of her wine and held the cool glass in her hands as she regarded him over the flickering light of the candle between them. "You're an enigma, you know."

His eyebrows lifted at that. "How so?"

"We're married, right? And we've spent months together, getting to know each other, and physically..." Her cheeks heated. "You know."

He nodded his head. "We've had a torrid love affair. I've done indescribable things to you. Things you should never tell your priest about."

She laughed softly and leaned forward. "Yeah, okay. But I still feel like you hold back a part of yourself from me."

His face grew more serious. "Is that why you want a divorce? Do you think I'm...keeping something from you?"

"Not like a secret or anything, just part of you."

The words caught in her throat as she finally expressed her fears. He was too good to be true. All of this — telling her that he loved her, bringing her to a surprisingly romantic place and sharing karaoke and a bottle of wine, supporting her eccentric nondenominational holiday festival aspirations — all of it was too good to be true. Because when she needed him most, he'd disappeared.

"Ask me anything," Ben said with a shrug. "Anything at all."

Anna licked her lips as she thought about it. "What's your favorite color?"

"Gray."

"Gray? No one's favorite color is gray."

"Mine is. What's your favorite color?"

"Purple. What did you want to be when you grew up?"

"A carpenter. My dad was a carpenter. Sawdust runs in my blood." He lifted his water. "Tell me your deepest secret."

Anna frowned at him. "No. This is supposed to be about you."

"Tell me your deepest secret and I'll tell you mine."

She chewed on her lower lip as she considered the question. "I'll tell you a secret. Not my deepest one."

Ben took an exaggerated breath and muttered, "Fine. Give me a deep secret."

Anna twisted the cloth napkin in her lap. She'd lived alone for most of her adult life. She had plenty of things to draw from. "Okay. All right. Here's one." She inched forward in her seat. "This one time I made myself a salad, and I was busy doing ten things at once and not paying attention. Anyway, I reached for what I thought were raisins and I sprinkled them on my salad, but they were really chocolate chips. And I ate the salad anyway, and you know what? It was delicious." She sat back triumphantly.

Ben tilted his head at her, unimpressed. "That's your secret? You like chocolate chips on your salad?"

What did he expect, that she was going to lead him to the location of a body or something? "I've never told anyone about that before. Chocolate and ranch dressing."

He wrinkled his nose at that. "That's not a secret, it's just disgusting."

"What can I say, I live a clean life. So, tit for tat. I get to hear your deepest secret now." She took a sip of wine.

Ben gazed at her, his eyes serious and somber. Then he said, "I was a male stripper."

She actually snorted wine out her nose and had to fumble for her napkin. "Stop it. You were not."

"I stripped my way through my carpentry apprenticeship. Money was tight, and I had to make ends meet."

115

Anna had no idea how he managed to keep such a straight face as he told her that. "Uh huh. Right."

He paused. "I'll prove it to you."

"What? No, you won't." He was so silly.

"Right now. I'll revive my act, live at The Barn."

He pushed back his chair and set off toward the stage. Anna watched him go, dumbfounded. He wouldn't really – oh, no. He was going to the DJ and flipping through the catalogue. When he took center stage and grabbed the mic, she covered her face with her napkin. Seconds later, the opening chords to "You Sexy Thing" began.

"This goes out to a special lady who showed me a good time tonight," Ben said, his voice low and sultry. He pointed across the room. "Darlene, my waitress." The server gave him a friendly wave. "Twenty percent tip, Darlene. You earned every penny." Seconds later, he broke into song.

His voice...was actually good. Ben was a great singer — how had Anna not known that? And his moves were so over the top, between his gyrating hips and the loosening tie, but she had to give him credit — it was still pretty sexy. By the middle of the song, when he was making his rounds of the restaurant and women were actually stuffing bills into his pockets, Anna was laughing so hard that she had to hold her sides. When the song ended, the crowd chanted for an encore, but Ben gave a melodramatic bow and explained that he had to get back to his dinner date. Then he walked offstage, leading with that cocky grin. "Well? Do you believe me now?"

"No. That was ridiculous." Anna swiped at her cheeks.

"Ah, well. I made six dollars just by loosening my tie." He pulled the crinkled bills from his pocket and set them on the table. "I'm pretty sure that makes me a professional now."

"You're a professional something, all right." Anna chuckled.

"Hey, nice performance." Darlene laughed as she came over to the table and handed them their dessert menus. "That's the first time anyone's ever dedicated a song to me."

Ben shook his head. "I don't believe it."

"It's true. So pick whatever you want. Dessert's on the house. For both of you." She patted him on the back. "I'll give you a few minutes."

Anna folded her arms across her chest in mock consternation. "You know exactly what you're doing."

Ben lifted his shoulders as he studied the menu. "I told you. Stick with me, kid."

She had to admit that he was making it very tempting.

After dessert, they shuffled off to the truck. This time, Anna had her arm wrapped snugly around Ben's waist, and he had his across her shoulders. He kissed her on the forehead. "I hope you enjoyed yourself tonight."

"I actually did."

"Shocking."

They paused beside the passenger door of the truck. The night air was crisp, the sky filled with stars. Anna looked straight above their heads. Through the vapor of her breath, she thought she could make out a red star. "The chocolate chip thing. That was a stupid secret," she whispered, and tucked her arms between their bodies for warmth. "I want to tell you a real secret."

This time there were no wisecracks from Ben, no clever retorts about the adequacy of her disclosures. He swept his fingers across her forehead to secure a lock of hair behind her ear. "I want to hear it." His breath brushed against her cheek.

"After you left, I started reading books on theoretical physics. Don't laugh," she said, even though he wasn't. "I found the theory of relativity comforting. The idea that time is an illusion, that everything that has happened or will happen is happening right now, but we can only perceive this moment. You and I are stardust, and we're newborns, and we're long dead, and everything in between, all at once." She felt her heart humming as she spoke. The possibilities left her breathless. "So we're together and apart at the same time, and we're married and strangers —"

Her voice broke off. Well, that last part didn't feel as theoretical. Anna swallowed and looked down at the space between them. "And we're happy. Somewhere in the universe, we are eternally happy." When she looked up again, her eyes were filled with tears. "That's my secret."

"That you take comfort in science?" His voice was soft, barely a whisper.

"That when you left, I was at my lowest point ever. And the only thing that made me feel better was thinking that somewhere, somehow, we were still happy."

That there was a place in the universe where they were still listening to their little girl's heart beating, filled with wonder and hope at the sound. Somewhere, Ben was constructing a crib and dreaming about the day he'd rock his baby to sleep. It still existed, even if she could no longer see it.

His face relaxed and he pulled her closer, stroking one finger along her jaw. "I would rearrange heaven and hell to make you happy. All you need to do is say the word. I will be with you, here, forever. We can travel back in time, Anna."

The words were sweet, but Anna knew the promise was broken before it was voiced. Knowledge changed everything — wasn't that lesson as old as Adam and Eve? There was no going back, not without a time machine. But there was the heat of Ben's body, and the thrill that shot across her skin every time he touched her cheek. There was tonight, and the fact that she'd spent two hours with him and managed to forget the ache just below the surface.

Yes, there was forgetting. That was something.

"Stay with me," she said, standing on her toes to whisper it in his ear. "Please. Just for tonight."

Because she was feeling weak, and like a child, and she was tired of taking care of everyone else. She left unspoken her deepest need at that moment: *Don't say "I told you so." Don't make this a joke.*

His blue eyes darkened until she thought she saw the need written in them. Reverently, he touched his fingers to the back of her head to pull her face toward his. Then he kissed her, sending heat through her veins with the sweetness of his lips. His beard was soft against her chin. He was perfect. "You're all I need," he said.

And she knew it was the truth.

When they reached her cottage, he carried her inside, just as he had on their wedding night, closing the door behind him with one foot. Anna slung her arms around his neck, her head resting on his shoulder, her lips nestled beside his ear. The cottage lights were off. "Do you still remember the way?" she asked.

"With my eyes closed."

He led her to the bedroom and set her down on the comforter, sliding off her coat before reaching for his own. His breath was jagged, and she marveled at the shaking of his fingers as he touched her. And she wanted to tell him how much she had missed him, and how much she had needed him, but that would have been remembering. All she wanted was to forget everything that made her hurt, if only for one night.

CHAPTER NINE

WHEN ANNA WOKE, he was still in bed beside her. He turned his head as she stirred and gave her a sleepy smile. "Morning, beautiful."

She stretched her arms and legs and rolled over onto her side, her limbs warm and heavy from sleep. "Were you able to sleep last night?" She was thinking of red wine, and how he'd told her it could keep him up. She didn't know whether white wine had the same effect.

Ben brushed her hair back from her face. "A little bit."

They were naked beneath the layers of bedding. Anna loved the soft scratch of cotton on her bare skin, but she almost always dressed heavily for bed in long pants and long-sleeved shirts. As she enjoyed the bristle of Ben's beard on her bare shoulder, she wondered why she covered up so much. Sometimes feeling was lovely. She managed to enjoy the moment for a few breaths, and then her mind began churning once again. Hedda's

Bakery would be by soon with platters of muffins, scones, and assorted cookies. She had a few guests checking out that morning and a surprising number checking in. Did Flossie have the rooms ready? She'd have to prepare the hot chocolate and cider before the skating rink opened, throw some logs in the fireplace —

"You need to go," Ben said. It wasn't a question.

She traced her finger down his beard. "Yes. I'm sorry. It's busy —"

"Shh, it's okay." He kissed her fingers. "When I'm in Archer Cove, it's your world and I'm just living in it."

He rolled onto his back as she rose and reached for her dress. It was Ben, and they were married, of course, but something about it felt new and uncertain. As she slipped the dress over her head and headed to the bathroom, Anna knew that she didn't regret sleeping with Ben, and she knew he felt the same. The sex had been unhurried and intense, oddly bereft of the humor they'd shared at The Barn. Almost sad, as if it might have been the last time.

Ben was gone when Anna emerged from the shower. She dressed, dried her hair, and hurried to the inn just as the Hedda's Bakery van was pulling up to the side. It was going to be a busy day, and she welcomed the distraction.

The refreshment stand was built in the style of a childhood lemonade stand, as a box with plywood walls, an opening on the side to serve as a door, and a little counter with a window in the front. Flossie had hastily painted "Refreshments" on a board and nailed it over the window. There was room enough for one person, possibly two, and a small table for food, thermoses, and cups. It did nothing to keep out the chill, and it only took the slightest edge off a brisk breeze coming in across the water. Basically it did the trick, but just barely.

Charis was manning the refreshment stand in a bulky violet wool knit hat and matching mittens. She waved excitedly as Anna approached and said, "Can you get over this turnout?"

Buses were parked in the inn's lot. Actual buses filled with people who wanted to attend the holiday festival to end all holiday festivals. Church buses, a senior citizen bus...even the neighboring town of Spencer was busing residents in from a satellite lot. Anna couldn't help but feel delightfully smug about the turn of events. "Sandy Thane is going to be spinning in her ugly red holiday dress. Also, this hot chocolate is amazing, if I do say so." It was her special recipe, a blend of dark chocolate, milk, heavy cream, and vanilla.

"Flossie's making another batch right now. I keep having to turn people away."

As if on cue, a little boy and his mother came up to the window of the stand. "Do you have any hot chocolate?" she asked hopefully.

"We're making more. If you come back in fifteen minutes, we'll have some." Charis leaned down to address the boy, who was wearing a blue knit hat with a pompom. "Would you like a sugar cookie, sweetheart?"

He got a big grin on his face. "Yeth pleath!" Anna smiled. He was missing his two front teeth.

Charis handed him a cookie and a small napkin and repeated her instructions to return in fifteen minutes. Then she turned to Anna and lifted her hands in the air as if to say, "See what I mean?"

Anna stuffed her mittened hands into her jacket pocket and looked around at the families gathered on the lawn. People of different ages and ethnicities were out together ice skating and building snowmen. "Who knew a holiday festival planned out of spite and a need for revenge could be so great?"

"If you'd asked me a week ago, I would've told you we were inviting bad karma," Charis said. "Looks like we pulled it off." She paused. "How did your date go?"

Anna kicked at a frozen clump of dirt with the toe of her boot. "Oh, fine. You know how Ben is. Mr. Charming."

Charis sensed her sister's hesitation. "But?"

"But nothing. I feel like he holds himself back from me." She lowered her voice, even though no one was waiting at the stand. "When I was pregnant, he was supportive, and he seemed like he was really excited about being a father. The minute we lost the baby, he was gone. He didn't want to talk about it or tell me what he was thinking about." Saying the words out loud dredged something up, and Anna blinked back tears. "When things are going well, he's great. Life of the party. And I think, this is a person I want to spend the rest of my life with. But when things were at the worst, he left."

Charis pressed her lips together thoughtfully as she considered Anna's words. "Maybe he has a different means of expressing himself."

"Charis." Anna tilted her head. "He took the baby crib out of the house while I was in the hospital. When I came home, every trace of our baby was gone."

Her sister frowned. "Did you ask him about it?"

"Yes. Sort of. All he would say was that he moved it out, and we didn't need it anymore." Anna swallowed the lump in her throat. "But I wanted to see that crib, you know?"

Charis nodded. "You wanted to grieve."

"It was all I had. I never saw her face. I only had that crib." Anna took a deep breath and swiped the back of her hand across her cheek. "I think I'm crying but I can't tell because it's so cold out. My face feels numb."

"Here, I'll get it." Charis gently wiped Anna's tears away with a napkin, but held her face for a moment longer between her hands. "You were a good mom, Anna. I know you loved her from the start."

That was it. She knew she was crying then. "Thanks, Char." No one had ever told her that before. She took a shaky breath. People were around, celebrating the holidays, and she needed to collect herself.

Charis reached up to smooth Anna's hair down her back. "You're both here now. Maybe you can work things out. Maybe an angel brought you two together for that reason."

Her sister believed in angels and rebirth and the healing power of crystals and essential oils. Basically,

Charis sampled from a buffet of spiritual beliefs. Anna had a difficult enough time with God. She laughed drily. "An angel named Flossie brought us back together." *Cheeky girl.*

"Are you talking about me again?" Flossie came up behind them, hauling two giant thermoses. "Better watch your mouths, 'cause Ben is only a few steps behind me."

Ben? Shoot. Anna was certain he'd panic once he saw the telltale signs of her crying episode: the red nose and eyes. Good Times Ben had managed to put the past behind him so easily. She both resented and envied him for it.

"Hey, Charis," he said, lumbering in with two more thermoses. "That's it. Four thermoses filled with hot chocolate."

"That oughta hold us for about five minutes," Charis mumbled. A line had already started to assemble in front of the window. "Don't get too comfortable, Flossie. I'm going to send you right back to the kitchen."

"I'll go," Anna said. "I'll leave now so we don't have to turn anyone away again."

She backed out of the stand quickly, trying to keep her head down and away, but Ben sought her out. "Hey. I haven't seen you all morning," he said as he caught up with her. "Impressive turnout. You must have hundreds of people here."

"I know, right?" She lowered her voice as she caught sight of a figure marching toward them across the grass. "Oh my gosh. It's Sandy Thane."

She looked a little bit like a headmistress in a long black jacket and matching gloves. And as always, she was smiling in a way that was a little bit frightening. "Well, well, Anna. Isn't this something."

She said it in the same tone one would use to marvel at a slightly disgusting scene, like, "Look at that giant spider devouring a fly. Isn't that something." Anna and Ben exchanged a quick glance and a small smile, and then Anna lifted her chin and said, "Why, thank you. Have you been to the refreshment stand? We have some hot chocolate —"

"I can't. My blood sugar." Sandy toyed with the top button on her coat and then tugged at the ends of her gloves, pulling them tightly against her fingers. "You know I've been trying to call you. I've left several messages." Her tone was sharp.

Anna looked her in the eye. "Yes. I know. I've been ignoring them."

Sandy recoiled slightly as if she'd been struck. "Oh."

"Look, I have things to do. My sisters and I have put a lot of time and thought into planning the festival, and we've added some new events, like this skating rink here."

"And the snow sculpture competition," Ben added.

"Right, and that. And it's going really well. And I realize that you've probably got your undies in a twist about all of this, you know, rebellion or whatever, but people are having fun here. So if you're here to enjoy yourself, then welcome. But otherwise, please scram."

Sandy clenched and unclenched her jaw and stood perfectly still. Finally she said, slowly, "It seems like a...nice...event."

What? Had Sandy really just given Anna a sort of compliment? She pressed her lips together and leaned forward ever so slightly. "Sorry, there's a lot of noise. I didn't quite hear that."

Sandy huffed and darted a gaze to the side. "I said that it seems nice. A nice event."

"Ah." Anna felt like springing into the air and turning cartwheels, but that would have been poor sportsmanship and undignified. Instead, she lowered her head in a little bow and calmly said, "Thank you. Please enjoy some complimentary hot beverages. We'd be happy to get you some unsweetened tea."

Sandy's eyes flew from Anna's face to Ben's and back again, but then she continued around them toward the skating rink. Anna waited until she was out of earshot before turning to Ben and gasping, "Oh my gosh. Did we just win?"

Ben chuckled. "If I'm not mistaken, that was Armageddon, right there. The final battle between good and evil."

"And I'm on the good side, right? I don't even care as long as I'm winning." Anna clapped her hands together and laughed. "You have no idea how gratifying that was."

"I think I have some idea." Ben stopped, his attention caught by something by the entrance to the property. "Uh oh."

"Uh oh? No, nothing can go wrong." Anna followed his gaze and caught a stream of flashing lights as several squad cars pulled into the parking lot. "No. Crap — what happened?"

Without another word, they took off in a sprint, flying around the groups of friends and families that were gathered across the lawn, dodging snowballs and skidding around snowmen, women, and children. Anna couldn't believe this. One, two, three — *four* squad cars? *Dammit.* She'd gotten smug too soon.

Their view of the activity was blocked by a wall of bodies gathering to observe the action. "Over here," Ben said, and tugged Anna's sleeve to lead her through an opening in the crowd.

When they came to the other side, Anna gasped and threw her hands over her mouth. "No!" she shrieked, and approached the nearest police officer. "What's going on here? This is my property!"

They had lined up a group of guests. Some were being patted down, and some already had their hands tied behind their back with plastic ties. "Are you arresting people?"

Oh, if Sandy saw this, Anna was toast.

"You're the owner?" The cop asked.

Hadn't she just told him that? "Yes. What's going on here?"

"This your party?"

Great, he'd mastered the art of not answering her questions directly. "Yes. Why? Are you arresting people?"

The cop took her by the arm. "Ma'am, I'm gonna have to ask you a few questions. Come this way."

Like she had any choice at all, the way he was tugging her. "What? Questions about what?" She looked over her shoulder for Ben, but he was following closely. "Am I under arrest? Do I need a lawyer?"

"You're not under arrest, ma'am. We just have a few questions."

"Anna, don't say anything!" Ben said.

Another cop came up and put a hand on Ben's chest, holding him back. "Sir, you're going to need to step over here."

"She hasn't done anything wrong! I'm her husband!"

Anna didn't hear the other cop's response as she stumbled down the driveway and toward a squad car. The cop opened the door and gestured. "You may want to get inside."

"Why? Are you taking me downtown?" It was just like on television.

He rolled his eyes. "No. But it's going to be a little while, so if you don't want to stand out here and freeze, then climb inside."

She gave it a moment of thought and then entered the car. It was barely warmer than the outside, but at least she could observe the action from a quieter spot. Anna watched the police officers search people and then lead them to squad cars. The crowd of onlookers grew, and it wasn't long before she noticed with dismay that Sandy Thane was among their numbers, her lips wrinkled into one angry little raisin.

Man, Anna thought as she slumped lower in her seat, out of view. *I hate the holidays.*

CHAPTER TEN

SOMEWHERE OVER ON the town green, people were decorating the tree with non-religious symbols of the season, and Santa was handing out solstice candy bars. In less than an hour, fireworks would be going off to honor the Chinese New Year. But Anna wouldn't see any of it, because hours after the arrests started, she was sitting in the warm lobby of the inn and explaining to two police officers why she was not responsible for the drug party that had spontaneously erupted on her front lawn.

Turns out a vanload of people had come to her holiday festival and started dropping ecstasy and who knew what else, right there on her front lawn. A rave. With people smoking things. She wanted to give up right then and there and lock herself in her room for a few days with some gossip magazines and a case of wine. Instead, she was dealing with Officers Martinez and Jones, who saw nothing funny about any of it.

Martinez held up a computer printout of a flyer. "Are you saying you didn't create this? Isn't this your email account?"

Anna squinted at the writing on the top of the page. "Yes, that's my account all right."

"But what you're telling us is that you didn't create this flyer, is that it?"

"No, my sis —" Anna stopped. Flossie was in charge of the advertising, but she wasn't about to give them a centimeter, and she certainly wasn't about to say anything that could get her little sister in trouble. "I don't see what's wrong with it. All it says is, 'Free Holiday Party.'"

They were sitting on the couches, Anna on the one closest to the fireplace, and the officers on the one beside it. Jones leaned in closer, crowding her personal space. "Ma'am, are you familiar with the term 'free party'?"

She looked from one to the other, pressing her hands together on her lap. What was this, some kind of prank? "It means free of admission." Right? Seemed obvious.

But no, this was not the million-dollar answer Officer Jones was looking for. "It means free of rules, ma'am," he said in a tone that revealed he believed she was stupid. "Free of law enforcement. A drug party."

"Oh," Anna said. Then, "*Oh.*"

"Yeah," Martinez laughed drily. "*Oh.*"

"This email message went out to several social media accounts we've been monitoring," Officer Jones explained. "So we had some undercover officers waiting here on-site when the van pulled up. Fortunately, we didn't have to wait long before the illicit activity started."

133

Illicit activity. On the front lawn of her inn. During her holiday festival. What a nightmare. "But you don't actually think I advertised a *rave* here. We had ice skating. It was a family event." She thought of Sandy Thane and her pursed lips, asking whether the event had taken on a PG-13 tone. Anna covered her face. "This is a terrible mistake. I didn't organize a drug party. No one did. I've never even smoked anything!"

"Unfortunately, you don't get brownie points for simply following the law, Ms. Tumblesby," Jones drawled. Anna was beginning to really dislike him.

"Listen, I can explain everything. My sister Charis really loves Christmas, right? And she roped me into planning this festival but she wanted me to do this news segment, but then my ex-husband walked in. Though I guess we're just separated, so —"

Martinez snapped his fingers. "Oh, wait! That was you! I saw that segment. There's this video out —"

She groaned. "The cat video. Yes. I know."

"No, there's this other one. I think it's penguins. Or puppies, maybe?"

He looked at Jones, who nodded without cracking a smile. "Puppies. It's puppies."

Martinez chuckled. "Yeah. It's clever. Really cute, too. But look," he said, his voice growing more serious again. "The good news is, we can't connect you with any illegal activity, other than this email." He waved the paper at her. "Most likely, it got into the wrong hands and went viral with the wrong people. So for now, we're going to assume you're telling the truth and that this was all some miscommunication."

Anna bit her tongue to keep from firing back a sarcastic *Gee, thanks!* "So I'm free to go?" She'd been watching too many crime shows on television.

"Yeah. For now," Jones added. "But we'll be watching you."

"Fine, whatever," she muttered.

Would they bug her house? Monitor her emails? Who knew, but this was not the time for questions. She needed a hot bath and a glass of wine, stat. Officers Tweedledee and Tweedledum needed to skedaddle.

She walked them to the front door, silently noting the puddles they'd tracked across her clean floors when they'd neglected to remove their boots. *First mop, then wine, then bath.* Jones stepped through the front door without another word. Clearly, to him, she was some criminal mastermind. But before Martinez left, he looked over his shoulder and gave a quick nod. "Merry Christmas." It was like the universe was laughing at her.

Outside on the front porch, she saw the alarmed faces of Ben and her sisters. Ben stepped forward as the officers exited. "Is everything finished?"

"We're all set," Martinez said. "Have a good night."

Anna held onto the door for support as the three rushed inside. Charis was the first to reach her. "Oh, Annie. What happened? We heard there were drugs?"

She rubbed at her temple and closed her eyes. Ben wrapped his arm around her waist to hold her upright. Thank goodness, because she was feeling pretty weak just then. "It was a mistake. Somehow a flyer was sent around —" She shook her head. "It doesn't matter. It wasn't anyone's fault, just some people taking advantage."

Ben led her to the couch, keeping his strong arm around her shoulders. She settled against him, feeling safe and protected. "H-how was the tree trim?" she said.

Flossie and Charis took a seat on the other couch. "It was okay," Flossie said, hesitating. "Fine."

"Only okay?" Anna said, suddenly alert. "Why, did something go wrong?"

"No, I think she's trying to spare your feelings." Charis leaned forward to set a hand on Anna's knee. "It was a lovely ceremony. Beautiful. We didn't stay for the fireworks, but people have had a great time."

"And Santa had the solstice bars, right?"

"Yes, everything was fine. Jessie brought them over just as she promised she would," Charis said.

"Oh, hey. I saved you a couple." Flossie reached into her handbag and brought out two brightly colored wrappers with silver metallic stars. "We have milk chocolate almond or dark chocolate sea salt."

Anna reached out a hand. "Sea salt, please." *First chocolate, then mop, then wine, then bath.*

Ben pulled her tighter and gave her a kiss on the forehead. "What can I do for you? Let me walk you home."

The tension in her muscles melted at the sound of his voice, but then she remembered the floors. "I have to mop the floors."

Charis regarded her with warmth in her eyes. "Why don't you go to bed, hon? Let me and Flossie take care of everything here."

She was too tired to argue. Ben helped her up and into her coat, and then they took the moonlit path to her cottage, holding hands the entire way. "I feel like I failed," she said. "Between the interview, and accidentally planning a rave...why can't I get anything right?"

"Come on, you're human. You're too hard on yourself."

She didn't feel human. She felt sort of victimized. "Everything that really matters, I manage to screw up."

"Anna." Ben looked at her. "That's not even remotely fair."

Fair? Fair didn't come into it. Life wasn't fair. "You know, you don't need to stay tonight," she said. "If you have somewhere else to be."

"Where do you think I would rather be?" The air filled with the sound of their boots on the walkway, and fireworks in the distance. "Why do you think I'd rather be somewhere else?"

"Seriously, Ben?" She dropped his hand to grasp her own head, frustrated by the madness of the question. "Maybe because you left me alone here? Remember, after we lost the baby?"

He halted and turned to face her, his face half-hidden in shadow. "I didn't leave you. I was here for a few weeks until you felt better. Then I was working."

"Until I felt better?" Her voice cracked. "It's been almost a year, and I'm still not sure I feel better. It still feels raw."

"How was I supposed to know that?" He threw his hands in the air.

"How could you *not* know that?"

She covered her face with her hands. All of a sudden, Anna felt heavy. Everything was all wrong, and it had been for a long time. And she was angry. So, so angry. "The problem with you," she said, fighting to maintain calm in her voice, "is that you can forget everything too easily. You walked away from me and our baby. All of it, just as easily as if you were heading to the next job. I was left here to deal with the physical and emotional pain of the loss. All alone."

In the light of the moon, she caught a flash of anger in his eyes. "Don't you think I grieved for her, too? The problem with *you* is that you can never let anything go. You never forget. But maybe your memory only works when it's convenient. Because *you're* the one who asked me not to come back."

Anna clenched her hands tightly as the rage she'd suppressed for so long, the anger she thought she was over, bubbled to the surface. "I asked you not to come back because you'd already left me alone. You were gone when I needed you the most. I fell in love with you because you made me laugh, but I see now that I never knew you. All those terrible nights...I never even saw you cry."

"I was trying to be strong for you."

"I didn't need you to be strong. I needed to know you remembered her and that you were hurting, too." Tears spilled out of her eyes, and she let them fall. "Don't you understand? I needed to know that she mattered to you, too."

"Anna." His voice softened. "Of course she mattered to me."

But she barely heard him above her own tears, and when he tried to pull her into his arms, she broke free. "No, it's too late. I've managed alone for too long. It's over."

She left him standing on the path, and he was wise enough not to try to follow. Anna entered the cottage and locked the door behind her. Then she undressed without bothering to find her pajamas. She slipped between the cool sheets and stared at the ceiling. Her heart hurt, and her eyes burned, but she had needed to say those words. Ben had a right to know how she felt. And deep down, Anna hated that she was spending her life making other people comfortable and happy, because she'd started to believe that happiness was reserved for everyone else.

But as she drifted to sleep, she thought that she wanted some happiness, too. Just a little bit. Maybe wrapped in a box, and sitting under her Christmas tree.

CHAPTER ELEVEN

IT WAS NO small Christmas miracle that the drug bust at the Archer Cove Inn hadn't put a damper on the rest of the holiday festival. Charis gave the credit to the alignment of the stars, but Flossie shrugged her shoulders and said, "Meh. Most of the people arrested were from out of town." It seemed as valid an explanation as any.

On Saturday night, people showed up to the Jingle Bell Dance at the community center. There was a disco ball in the center of the room and a deejay who had somehow created an electronic dance mix out of classic Christmas carols, but guests still enjoyed themselves. Anna thought it was remarkable. "As holiday dances go, it's a little bit over the top," she said to Charis and Flossie as they hung out in the back of the room, enjoying the spiked eggnog. "The deejay is wearing antlers strung with lights."

"I think it's fun," Flossie said. "People seemed to enjoy the candy cane limbo."

"I agree, that was a nice touch." Charis's eyes were wide and sincere. She'd had too much eggnog. "Everything I've heard has been positive."

"Great. Well, I'm sorry we didn't ruin the festival for you, Charis," Anna said as she looped her arm with her sister's. "Maybe next year."

"Did I tell you? Sandy Thane said I could plan it again. She apologized and everything." Charis hesitated. "Did you want to plan it, too?"

"Honestly? No. No way." Anna snorted as she took a sip of her drink.

"Oh, good. Because Sandy said that she would feel more comfortable if there was only one chair of the committee, so..."

Anna had to laugh at that. "I'll bet. No, Char, that's fine. It's all yours."

All the eggnog, candy cane limbo, and antler hats in the world weren't going to change Anna's mind. She was pleased she'd managed to plan a successful festival, but she was also disappointed at what hadn't happened. Two days before Christmas, and she was still feeling that nagging emptiness that had followed her all season. She'd thought that keeping busy was the answer, and there she was with an inn filled with guests and more activity than she could manage, and none of it had worked. At that point, she was resigned to disliking the holidays. Spring would come soon enough.

The inn cleared out on Sunday morning. Anna would close the inn for the Christmas holiday, and she needed the break to recover. After the last guest checked out, she and Flossie cleaned the rooms and sat down to enjoy some tea in front of the fire. "Cheers, little sister," Anna said as she lifted her mug of peppermint tea. "What would I have done without you these past two weeks?"

"Clink clink." Flossie blew steam over the top of her mug. "I can't believe it's Christmas Eve. Or that Mom and Dad are spending it on a cruise."

Anna laughed. "They'll be home in a few days and we'll all celebrate it then. Plus, I kind of like the idea of having Christmas with you and Charis. We can bake muffins and stay in our pajamas all day if we want to." A low-maintenance Christmas sounded just delightful. "Maybe I'll get into the holiday spirit yet."

"I want to spend the day watching old movies and napping on the couch." Flossie propped one slippered foot up on the ottoman and took a cautious sip of her tea. "Have you heard from Ben?" she asked quietly.

Anna pulled a red-and-white knit throw onto her lap. "No." Somewhere around her heart, it still ached. "It's for the best. I put it all on the line and told him everything I've been carrying around for so long...and he left. Ben leaves."

They sipped their tea and listened to the crackle of the logs in the fireplace. Outside, the evening was cold and dark, and families were taking comfort in their holiday traditions. Anna might be at a low point, but she could still count her blessings, and she was very blessed, indeed. She reached over to touch her sister's hand. "I'm glad you're here with me. I'm lucky to have you in my life."

142

Flossie squeezed her hand back. "I have something for you. I hope — is it okay for me to give it to you?"

"Yeah, of course."

"It's just, I wasn't sure because..." Her voice trailed off. "Wait here."

She set her tea down and jumped up to run upstairs. A moment later she came back, carrying a small box wrapped in shiny red paper. "I don't want you to be upset. It's little, but..." Flossie set the package on Anna's lap and tugged nervously at her hair. "Too late now, so just open it."

Anna slipped her fingers beneath the seams of the paper and tugged the tape loose. Inside was a white cardboard box. When she lifted the lid and removed a ball of tissue paper, she saw a little silver bell tied with a bubblegum pink ribbon. "It's for the baby," Flossie said softly. She swallowed, and her chin trembled. "I bought it for her when I found out you were expecting, and I wanted you to still have it. I just wish things were different, Annie. I'm so sorry."

Anna turned the bell over in her fingers. It made a sweet, soft ring as it moved. "I love that you thought of her."

"I don't always know the right things to say. Like, I don't know how to make you and Ben feel better. So all I can say is that I won't ever forget her. She mattered to me, and a part of me will always feel a little bit sad that I never met her."

Anna's breath rattled as she inhaled. "That's the perfect thing to say." She leaned over to hug her. "Thank you."

"Love you. Merry Christmas." Flossie gave her a kiss on her hair and sat back down. After a pause, she said, "You know, Ben grieved too. We talked about it a lot while he was here. He did it in his guy way." She waved a hand vaguely. "Pretending that he was fine so that he would be strong for you. But if you ask me, he's been tortured. He's lost without you."

"Uh huh," Anna murmured tightly as she rang the little bell. "Well, I don't —"

"I'm just saying," Flossie said, and lifted her hands in the air. "I'm not meddling. I learned my lesson the hard way. Anyway, Charis will be by soon with a pizza from Meme's."

"That sounds delicious." Anna sighed. She didn't feel like cooking. "What would Christmas Eve be without pizza, anyway?"

"I'm going to make you believe in Christmas yet." Flossie winked. "Just you wait."

The three sisters ate pizza and watched *It's a Wonderful Life* before retiring to their room. Every Christmas Eve since Anna had purchased the inn, they had camped out in the largest guest suite. Anna cherished the tradition more that year than in any other. Being alone suddenly felt unbearable.

She drifted off to sleep and awoke to creaking downstairs. She opened one eye and reached for her watch. Four thirty. *Must be the house settling.* She rolled over in bed.

The floor creaked again.

Anna sat upright. Charis was asleep beside her. Flossie was snoring on the pull-out bed. Anna sat perfectly still, clutching the comforter to her chest. Another creak. Definitely footsteps.

She swallowed and slowly set one foot on the floor. *I should call the police.* Yeah, right. And with her luck, Jones and Martinez would show up. Anna reached for her bathrobe and pulled it on. She slipped an iron poker from the set beside the fireplace and clutched it tightly in her fists. *Christmas Day burglary. Just dandy.*

Inch by inch, she tiptoed down the hall and peeked into the lobby. Someone had left a large package wrapped in a giant red bow — what the heck? Anna's heart raced as she took bolder steps down the staircase. When she reached the bottom, Ben was standing beside the couch. Waiting for her. "Merry Christmas, Anna," he said. Then he noticed the poker in her hand. "Are you going to hit me?"

"Possibly." But she relaxed her arm. "What are you doing here?" She reached for a lamp and flicked it on. There were still a couple hours before sunrise.

"I'm leaving. But I wanted to bring you your gift first." He walked over to the large package. "Open it."

It was oddly shaped and wrapped in shiny white paper. The red bow was as large as her head, but it tore easily away. Anna pulled off the paper and took a step back. Her voice caught in her throat. She recognized it immediately, but she couldn't speak.

"Do you know what it is?" Ben asked after a few moments had passed.

Anna nodded mutely, her hands clapped over her throat. "Yes." Her voice was hoarse, her throat pinched.

It was the headboard of the crib. The white, gently arched curves that she'd run her fingers across so many times. He'd turned it into the back of a bench, and he'd used the bars of the crib to join it to the seat. Anna touched it carefully, almost afraid it might vaporize before her.

"I didn't know what to do with it," Ben said. "I was just...lost, I guess. I put it in my parents' woodshed. I couldn't even look at it. I mean, I built it for her. It was supposed to be her crib." He scratched at the back of his neck. "Then when I came back here, I thought, I know what I'll do. I'll make a bench, and you can put it in your garden, and every time you go out there, you will think of her. Go ahead," he said as Anna hovered over the seat. "Sit down. It's sturdy."

Anna sat. She touched the smooth arm of the bench. "It's just gorgeous," she whispered. "So this is where you've been when you disappeared? You've been working on this?"

"Yeah. A few hours here and there. I told Flossie about it. Glad she kept a secret."

"For once." Anna patted the spot next to her. "Please. Sit next to me."

146

He hesitated for a second, but then sat. Anna reached over to hold his hand. "When we came home from the hospital and the crib was gone, I thought you threw it away. I didn't know what to think."

Ben looked down at their hands. "I didn't know what to do. I thought it might be easier for you that way. I should've asked."

"*I* should've asked," Anna said. "I was so hurt and angry at the world, I guess."

"Can I tell you something? My deepest secret?" He turned to her, his eyes wide and earnest. "When we lost the baby, it scared me to death. I didn't know how to reach you. I couldn't make you laugh anymore. I wanted you to stop hurting. Then you asked me to leave, and it was like you'd opened this escape hatch." He pulled her hand up to kiss her fingers. "I love you so much, Anna. I shouldn't have run. All I wanted was to fix you. I didn't know how. I'm so sorry."

There was something new in his face, as if he'd lifted a veil and shown her the deepest part of him. She saw it in his pain and vulnerability. She *saw* him, all of him. And he was beautiful.

"I love that you told me that," she whispered. "I've always been afraid of trapping you. I want you to be here because you want to be."

"I want to be here." He wrapped his arm around her shoulders and pulled her closer to his side. "What happened before, the leaving... There's plenty of work for me around Archer Cove. I want to be with you."

"I like that idea." She leaned her head against his shoulder. "Thank you for making this bench. To honor her. It means more to me than you'll ever know."

They sat together for some time in the semidarkness of the morning, listening to the steady tick of the clock in the lobby. Eventually Ben said, "I feel bad that we never named her. There was never a birth certificate. No one ever asked."

"I always thought her name should be Eva."

"That's pretty. What's it mean?"

"Life."

Ben nodded slowly. "I like that."

He kissed the top of her head as she snuggled in against him. He smelled like sawdust and soap. He felt like home. "I'm glad you didn't wrap up divorce papers," she said. "Because I really do love you. And the fact that you love me too, well... that's amazing, considering I'm not always the easiest person to love."

"It's always been easy for me." He rested his chin on the top of her head. "Do you think we can give it another try? Marriage, I mean. I swear, honey. I know we got off to a rough start, but the best is ahead of us."

"I know it is."

"So that's a yes?"

"Yes, or I do...whatever. I missed you. I'm glad you came back. Merry Christmas."

"Merry Christmas, sweetheart."

She rested her hand against Ben's chest to feel his heartbeat. And Anna knew that right then, in that space and time, sitting with Ben under the Christmas tree, she was truly happy.

* * * * *

A Note from the Author

THANK YOU FOR taking the time to read A WINTER PROMISE! Reviews help readers to connect with books they might enjoy. If you are so inclined, an honest review at the site of your choice would be appreciated. If you are interested in hearing about new releases, please sign up for my newsletter on my website at http://nataliecharlesromance.com.

I've realized that in the darkest times, I see the most angels. I thought of you while writing. To all of those who touch lives with kindness, thank you. And special thanks to fellow author and dear friend Olivia Miles, who has been with me through thick and thin, high and low. Finally to my copy editor Amanda Sumner, who makes each of my books better and does so without laughing at me — thank you.

About the Author

NATALIE CHARLES HAS worked as an attorney, a playground supervisor, and a makeup sales clerk, but not in that order. The happy sufferer of a lifelong addiction to mystery novels, Natalie has, sadly, never out-sleuthed a detective. She is a RT Reviewer's Choice Award winner and has been a finalist for the Daphne du Maurier Award for Mystery/Suspense. She lives in Connecticut with her hero husband and two bookish children.

Natalie loves connecting with readers! You can find her on Facebook, facebook.com/writernataliecharles or Twitter @tallie_charles, or you can contact her through her website, nataliecharlesromance.com; or email at writernataliecharles@gmail.com.